"I love you," he said in a thick voice.

"I've loved you since that afternoon I first saw you. I hadn't even been praying to meet anyone. It just happened, with God's timing. Sometimes He kinda zaps you when you least expect it."

"But you can't move here, Leighton. It wouldn't work out."

"Why not?"

Alice moved her hand. "I can't let you do it. If I agreed to this move, you'd regret it. The bay is in your blood. Your work is there—your home, the cannery. I can't let you give that up."

"My mind's made up. I'm going to do it."

"And I say it's wrong." Her voice rose as she looked away. She couldn't look him in the eye. Not now.

BIRDIE L. ETCHISON lives in Washington State and knows much about the Willamette Valley, the setting for the majority of her books. She loves to research the colorful history of the United States and uses her research along with family stories to create wonderful novels.

Books by Birdie L. Etchison

The Sea Beckons

Birdie L. Etchison

Heartsong Presents

With Love and Blessings to my five granddaughters:
Tawnisha, Jennifer, Samantha, Laura, and Tabitha

A note from the author:
*I love to hear from my readers! You may correspond with me
by writing:* **Birdie L. Etchison**
Author Relations
PO Box 719
Uhrichsville, OH 44683

ISBN 1-58660-153-9

THE SEA BECKONS

Scripture taken from the HOLY BIBLE: NEW INTERNATIONAL VERSION®.
NIV®. Copyright © 1973, 1978, 1984 by International Bible Society.
Used by permission of Zondervan Publishing House.

All of the characters and events in this book are fictitious. Any
resemblance to actual persons, living or dead, or to actual events
is purely coincidental.

Cover illustration by Jocelyne Bouchard.

PRINTED IN THE U.S.A.

one

Alice Adams sat in the office waiting for the phone to ring. It had been a slow morning, as Wednesdays often were. Two stacks of envelopes were ready to mail. One stack was invoices for the month of May for Spencer Computer Consultants, and the other was an advertisement for a sale on good, used computers. The back room had computers on the table, in all corners, and one chair held an old daisy wheel printer.

"Totally obsolete," Steven had said, "but you never know. We may be able to use some parts."

Alice glanced at the clock. Courtney, her daughter and only child, was at the obstetrician's office for a checkup and an ultrasound to determine her baby's gender. Alice preferred the old way of waiting until the baby's birth to know the sex. It was something to look forward to, but then nobody had asked her. She went along with whatever Courtney wanted. And one good way to look at it was she would know what color sweater to knit. The baby was expected November 21, a month before Courtney and Steven's first anniversary.

She was glad they had wanted a baby right away. Nothing could have made Alice happier. She'd so longed for a baby when she and Carl had first married, but it wasn't in God's plan. After several miscarriages, they'd decided to adopt, and Courtney was that child. Now Alice would be a grandma, and she could hardly contain her excitement.

Jeff whistled out in the hall. She knew it was Jeff because he always whistled "Puff the Magic Dragon." He was her son-in-law's right-hand man, and she was quite fond of him. He had a nice sense of humor and was respectful. So many young people weren't these days. But at fifty, Alice was "out of touch," as some put it.

"Hey, Mrs. Adams. I mean, Alice! I found a customer when I was at Maxson's." She had asked him to call her Alice, but he usually forgot.

"Oh, really?" She smiled. "As if you needed to drum up business."

"Yeah. My friend's father is visiting, and his laptop stopped working. I have it here. He'll stop by later this afternoon to pick it up."

Steven didn't need more customers; he was far busier than he wanted to be. He had put an ad in Sunday's Help Wanted column, looking for a second employee. Jeff had decided he wanted Saturdays off, imagine that. And of course Steven wanted to spend more time with Courtney and the baby who would soon join their family.

The phone rang. Alice leaned over, catching it at the end of the first ring.

"Spencer Consultants—"

"Mom, it's me!"

Alice drew in a quick breath. "So you know what the baby is and everything's okay?"

"Yes, we're having—"

"No, don't tell me," Alice interrupted. "I want to wait until I see you in person. Maybe we can have a cup of coffee. Or is it orange juice you're drinking these days?"

"Mom, what say we take a walk over by Meier & Frank during your lunch break?"

Alice chuckled. "That doesn't have anything to do with the fact that they have one of the largest baby departments, does it?"

"Mom, no! Of course not. I don't suppose Steven is there?"

"No, Honey, he has that job over on Swan Island. Said he'd be gone until five or so."

"I wish he could have come to the doctor's with me, but we'll celebrate tonight."

Alice looked out the window at the view over the Willamette. The river was still high from spring rains. The river ran through the downtown area, going north and south. A jet ski zipped by. Later in the day, pleasure boats would fill the water. A barge now moved slowly past. Usually offices with a view would be too costly, but Steven got a good deal because he knew the owner and was on his payroll to keep all his computers up and running.

"I'll meet you in an hour on the corner; that is, if Jeff will let me leave then."

Jeff's head shot up at the sound of his name. "I bet you and Courtney are going to buy out the baby store."

Alice tried to look shocked. "Jeff, how could you possibly think such a thing?"

She told her daughter good-bye. Jeff was writing on a business card and now held it up. "I say the baby's a boy!"

"You have a 50 percent chance of being right."

"Yeah, so I do." He bent back over the laptop.

Alice took a moment for a silent prayer of thanks. Thanks that Courtney had carried her child this long. It was a good indication. But since Courtney was not her natural child, there was no reason not to believe she'd have a full-term pregnancy.

She straightened her short salt-and-pepper hair and rose to get a cup of coffee. So much had happened in one short year. God had answered many prayers. If only Carl were here to feel this joy.

"There. I had an idea that would be it." Jeff cut through her thoughts. He was in the workroom, a large room with one big table and several smaller tables, all containing computers in various stages of being fixed.

"It just needed a good cleaning where the plug goes in. People never think about it. It's sort of like cleaning the ear-wax out of your ear. Here, call Leighton. He can pick it up anytime."

Jeff handed Alice a card. *Leighton Walker. Oysterville, Washington.*

"Oysterville? What's he doing here?"

Jeff shrugged. "Here on business, I guess. All that I know

is he's an oysterman."

"An oysterman?"

"You know what oysters are. Someone has to grow them."

"They don't grow them, do they?"

"It's quite a process. You don't dig them like you do clams or fish for them like other seafood."

"I didn't know." She dialed a local number. A deep voice answered immediately.

"This is Alice at Spencer's Computer Consultants, and I have Mr. Walker's laptop ready."

"Yeah, that's me. Now that's what I call speedy. You say I can come pick it up now?"

"Anytime, Mr. Walker."

She gave directions to the downtown office. She wondered if he would arrive before she left to meet Courtney.

She had just reached for her lightweight jacket after adding lipstick to full lips—her Carl had always said she looked like she was pouting—when the knock sounded. Instinctively, Alice adjusted her skirt and collar. It was a nervous habit. She always wore a tailored suit to the office, though Steven said she could dress casually.

"Yes?"

"I'm Leighton Walker. Came to pick up my laptop."

Alice shivered unexpectedly as a pair of deep brown eyes met hers. It was as if in that second, Carl was smiling at her. He was the same height as Carl, a good six foot three. At five-nine, Alice felt more comfortable around tall men. But it was the crooked smile that made her face flush.

"Is there something wrong?"

He looked puzzled and Alice had to laugh. "Oh, my, no. It's just that you remind me of someone."

"I'm not from around here."

"I know." She held up his card. "It says right here you're from Oysterville."

His frown disappeared as he appeared to relax. "Good deduction."

Jeff stuck his head around the corner. "It was like I thought. Just needed a cleaning."

"Well, Jeff, I sure appreciate this. Most places take a week or more. How much do I owe?" Leighton removed a wallet from his back pocket.

"Ten is fine."

"Ten? That's nothing."

"Only took me ten minutes." Jeff plugged the laptop in. "See, it comes right on. No problem."

Leighton extricated a ten-dollar bill and handed it to Alice. She was already writing him a receipt.

He folded it and placed it inside his wallet. A woman with a smile stared out of the top picture in the picture part of his wallet.

"Who do I remind you of?" he asked then.

Alice felt the color rise to her cheeks again as she looked away. "My late husband, Carl."

"Oh."

She nodded and pushed her chair in. "Yes. It's been five years now."

"I know about loss. I lost my daughter three years ago. Cystic fibrosis."

"I'm sorry to hear that."

"Hannah lived longer than most with CF because of her stubbornness. She was so determined and fought the illness with everything she had. She was the youngest of my five."

"Five!" The word slipped out before Alice could stop it.

"Five? Yes." He looked at her with a perplexed expression. "Does that surprise you?"

Alice smiled inwardly, thinking of how long she had wanted just one child. What a blessing to have two, but five? She wondered if she could have handled five.

"I just have one. Courtney," she said finally.

"I guess five sounds like a lot. And believe me it is when they all get together." A shadow crossed his face for a fleeting moment.

"And where are your children now?"

"Two live on the peninsula. Luke, my oldest son, helps me run the sea farm up in Oysterville. Tom teaches math in the high school, and John lives here. Not sure about my youngest son, Aaron. He's off somewhere, doing his own thing."

And who is the mother of these children? Alice wanted to ask.

As if reading her mind, Leighton added, "My wife died some years ago now."

"I'm sorry, but your children are a blessing to you."

"For sure."

He handed her a card that showed the peninsula, a long thin strip of land surrounded by the Columbia River, Willapa Bay, and the Pacific Ocean. "I live about as far north as you can go. It's beautiful there."

Alice wanted to talk longer, but needed to leave. "I'm sorry, but I'm meeting my daughter and better not be late. She's having a baby, my first grandchild, in less than five months."

"Hey, congratulations!" His eyes crinkled up on the end as he held the door open. "I'll ride down in the elevator with you."

Alice had heard of people falling in love at first sight, but she'd never believed it was possible. She didn't believe it to be possible now, yet, there was something, a magnetism between them. His eyes seemed to smolder, his gaze meeting hers head-on. This was one of those times when she missed Carl. Missed his comforting arms, holding her close, the feel of his strong body, his thick, muscular shoulders. Why was she feeling this way now? And why was this man staring at her? She knew he was, though she hadn't met his gaze again. She hadn't dared. She could imagine what Courtney would say about all of this.

"Here we are." The elevator door opened and he stepped out, waiting for her to exit. "Alice, isn't it?"

She nodded, her face burning again, almost as if she was embarrassed.

"I have not looked at a woman since Hannah's death, but something inside me is urging me to ask you out. Could I drop by and take you to lunch tomorrow since today is taken up?"

"I haven't dated, either," she heard herself saying. Her hand went to her hair. "I don't think I should start now."

"This is irregular, I know, and you don't know me, but trust me when I say I don't go around asking women out. But sometimes you just want to talk to someone over a lunch of clam chowder and breadsticks."

Alice laughed then. "Clam chowder? How did you know that's my favorite?"

He shrugged. "I didn't. That's good, isn't it?"

"I suppose it is."

They were out on the sidewalk, though Alice couldn't remember walking down the hall to the main door of the building.

"I'll walk with you to where you're meeting your daughter, if that's okay."

Alice fell in step with the attractive man, unable to believe she had talked to him as if he was an old friend.

"How about if I stop by at noon tomorrow?"

Then she remembered. She wasn't going in tomorrow. Steven planned on being in the office all day, so Alice had the day off.

"I'll be at the hospital. I volunteer mornings."

"Well, maybe another time when I'm in town."

He looked so disappointed that without thinking it over, Alice blurted out, "I could meet you at one o'clock. Say, the library."

He had impulsively taken her hand, just as Courtney walked up the block.

"Mother?" Courtney said, as if she couldn't believe this was her mother standing on a street corner of downtown Portland with a man. A nice-looking man.

Alice smiled as Leighton stepped forward, extending his hand.

"Hello, I'm Leighton Walker, a client, and you're Courtney. Congratulations on the baby. We were just talking while we waited for you."

Courtney finally shook his hand. "I—that is—thank you." She looked imploringly at her mother, but Alice said nothing.

"We're having lunch tomorrow. Do you want to come?"

Courtney was silent.

"It's probably not a good idea," Alice said, breaking in. "I don't think—"

"I'll be waiting at one. The library steps."

They watched while he turned and disappeared around the corner of Fifth and Madison.

"And now, are you going to tell me about the baby?" Alice reached over and pushed a tendril of hair from her daughter's cheek, eager to change the subject. "If only your father were here to rejoice in this awesome occasion."

Courtney narrowed her eyes. "Mom, Dad *is* here. I feel his presence a lot. Now, are you going to tell me who that man is?"

"His son is Jeff's friend, and he's here visiting, and he came in and, oh, I don't know. It all happened so fast—"

"Mother, you don't even know him. I'm sure Steven would feel as appalled as I am right now."

"What!" Alice's voice was almost shrill. "I'm not a child. Why should you feel appalled?"

"Mom, it's a different world now than when you dated Dad. You can't trust people."

"I can trust my own instincts, and I know Leighton Walker is a very nice man. Now, are we going to go shopping or what?"

But even as she said it, Alice knew the conversation would not be about the expected baby, but more about her lunch date.

two

Leighton Walker hurried up the block, his long strides full of confidence as he thought of the woman he had just met, the look of near shock on her daughter's face. Well, he felt that same shock inside him now, although a different kind. He liked this woman. Her voice had a happy sound. Or was it her laugh? She was going to mean a lot to him; it was as if God had opened a door, and this time he wasn't about to slam it.

He had made the trip to Portland to woo potential customers. He'd opened the Sea Gifts Store the year Hannah died. Now customers could come in and buy six or a dozen fresh oysters. He also had canned and smoked oysters and offered oyster stew. It was something he'd always wanted to do. Just last week he'd added a variety of spices and books by local authors. Things were selling well.

Oysters were a succulent treat to most, but Hannah had disliked them. "One thing about oysters, Daddy," she'd said after a night of a bad attack, "you either love 'em or hate 'em."

He had held his fragile child close. *Oh, Lord, help me to face the inevitable.*

Hannah had lain back down. "Daddy, I know you are praying. I can always tell." She giggled. "You get that furrow in your brow and your mouth relaxes."

"Is that so?" He pulled the covers up under her chin, thinking once again how much she looked like her mother, Nancy. Nancy with the laughing eyes, dimples, and mischievous grin. Nancy, whom he had known all his life.

He wondered why his heart had suddenly lurched at the sight of the tall, lean woman with dark eyes and short curly hair in the computer office. Had it been the depths of her eyes or the smile that filled up every inch of her face? He'd not seen a smile like that in a long, long time.

Without a second thought, he'd felt a nudge and had spoken to her about lunch. *It was crazy,* he thought now as he leaned back in the chair. He always stayed at John's high-rise apartment when he came to Portland. He had come to try to sell his line of canned oysters to two of the main seafood restaurants in town. He had two appointments this afternoon. How would it come out? A peace and sudden warmth filled him. If it worked, it did. If it didn't, it didn't. Leighton had learned at a young age that one had to roll with whatever life gave you. When his child was born sick, he turned to Nancy with a nod.

"We'll love her, Nance. Cherish her and protect her and do what has to be done."

"Easy for you to say," had been her comeback. She looked up at him out of listless eyes. "I prayed so hard for a girl. I didn't think I had to pray for one to be healthy." She turned away. "I didn't think God would be so cruel, Leight, to send us one with an affliction like this."

"God is never cruel."

"He was this time."

"No, Nance, you have it wrong."

It had hurt to see her unwilling to accept the challenge, to care for the baby who so needed her mother's loving touch.

Nancy had tried for a year, then left. Luke, at twelve, did not understand at all why his mother moved out of the house. The other three seemed to take it more in stride. She met them after school and took them for ice cream, or they'd walk the beach. But she didn't come home to see Hannah, nor would she answer Leighton's calls.

They had never divorced, though he knew she dated other men. Then she left the peninsula and sent notes and cards to the boys. Again, she did not include Hannah.

She had died by her own hand three years later. He'd prayed for her soul, knowing she had been tortured and couldn't have been in her right mind to do such a thing.

He'd been alone twenty years, throwing himself into his

work. His children were his whole life, especially after Nancy left. He had tried to be both mother and father. Then Aunt Rita came to help out, and he'd been thankful. She had pounded Hannah's back when the mucous was so thick she could not breathe. Together they worked and prayed for the frail child. Aunt Rita invented games that were quiet, read a multitude of books, they finger-painted garish orange and purple pictures, doing whatever was needed for her small, sick niece. Recently he'd heard about new treatments and lung transplants for CF patients, but the news had come too late for Hannah.

Back at John's apartment, Leighton looked out at the view of Mount Hood, a glorious snowcapped peak. His heart swelled nearly shut. So many things had happened in his life. At eleven, he'd been miraculously saved after a sudden squall and his canoe capsized in the bay. He'd disobeyed by going out alone without permission. After clinging to the canoe for an hour, he'd been rescued by a crabbing boat. The spanking he expected was not administered by his father or mother. Two things he remembered from that day: his mother who couldn't stop crying and his belief that there had to be a Supreme Being who took care of small boys who did fool-hardy things.

When his sick daughter was born, Leighton had dug in his heels and coped. Then Aaron strayed from the fold, and Leighton had no idea where he was now. The boy, a happy-go-lucky child, had made everyone laugh. He had more of Nancy in him than Leighton ever realized. Each day began with a prayer for Aaron. And, of course, his other three sons. God was the main force in his life. God was there, Someone to cry out to, to pray to, to lean on in tough times. But never had he thought of another helpmate. He'd been making it okay, hadn't he? Then today he met Alice.

"Lord, have You given me a sign today? Are You telling me I should pursue this woman? I can't believe I had enough nerve to ask her out for lunch."

He thought about the verse in Psalms that said, "Great peace have they who love your law, and nothing can make them stumble."

The phone rang, breaking through Leighton's reverie. It was John.

"Dad, I have tickets to the Pops concert tonight, but I'm driving down to Salem. Haven't found anyone who can use them. How about you?"

"What would I do with two tickets?"

"You must know someone else in town."

Leighton's mind flashed to Alice. She seemed to be the type that would enjoy a concert. "Yeah, I'll take them off your hands."

"Good. I'll drop them by before I leave."

Leighton sat back and wondered if Alice would agree to the concert. This seemed more like a date than lunch tomorrow.

He'd been out of practice so long. He smiled. He'd never practiced even back in the beginning. He and Nancy had attended the same church, the youth group, and went on all the functions. They just sort of started dating when they were both seventeen. And nature had taken its course. He had never looked at another woman, not really looked. Friends tried to pair him up after Nancy's death, but he was too busy with work and taking care of his kids. There'd been no one, unless he counted Cora.

He showered and took his one good suit from the hanger. He had wondered about dressing casual for this meeting with the restaurant owners but decided against it. He might be a beach bum, but he didn't want to look like one.

An hour later, he sat across from the man who signed on the dotted line for his next order of oysters, then Leighton talked about the new products. "You can sell the canned oysters right in the restaurant. Offer them some of our new spices. Soon your customers will be clamoring for them."

They rose, shook on the deal, and Leighton left, his head held high. "Wow, Lord, that one was easy. Now, if my phone call to Alice comes off as easily."

He was back at the apartment. The screen on his laptop, a purchase of just two years ago, sat staring at him. Fish of all sizes and colors bobbed up and around on the screen, mesmerizing him. He started to dial the number then hung up.

"Ah, why don't I just go ahead and call? If she says no, the sun still rises tomorrow morning."

Alice had gone home and he got Jeff.

"She just works mornings most of the time. If it looks like a busy week, like after an ad comes out, Steven asks her to come in for the whole day."

"I suppose it's against protocol to give me her home phone number."

There was a pause. "Well, I suppose not. You are a client, after all."

Seconds later, Leighton was once more dialing a number. On the third ring an answering machine kicked in. Of course. She probably hadn't gotten home yet. He'd call again in an hour or so.

&

Courtney finally told her mother she was carrying a boy.

Alice hugged her close. "I'll like having a grandson. Of course this means Jeff wins. He said it was a boy."

"I can't wait to see Steven's face. He's going to rush out to buy a football. Just you watch."

They meandered through the baby department, and Alice bought fuzzy blue sleepers, blue receiving blankets, and a quilt that was definitely for a boy. "Isn't this fun?"

"I won't have enough room in the apartment if you buy like this every time you get close to a store."

Alice nodded. "You're right. Let's call it a day."

After calling to check with Jeff, Alice decided to go on home. She had things to mull over, baby clothes to look at again, a lunch date for the next day.

An hour later, after taking Max, the local transit, to Parkrose, Alice lugged her purchases to her car. She often stopped at the grocery store but wanted to go straight home today.

The light blinked on her telephone as she dropped the packages on the bed.

"Who would be calling?" she said aloud, her mind always going to Agnes, her sister.

A male voice boomed into the room. "Leighton Walker here. We met earlier today. I'm the one with the ailing laptop."

She trembled as she glanced at her face in the mirror over the dresser. "He's calling me? But why?"

"Have two tickets for the Oregon Pops concert tonight. Just wondering if you'd go with me. Don't know anyone else in town and thought it might be fun. I'll call you back around four."

A Pops concert. She loved the group. And she hadn't been to a concert in years. She couldn't return the call, as he hadn't left a number. She hoped he wouldn't ask someone else.

She looked in the kitchen for leftovers. There was a chicken drumstick and a bit of the Jell-O left from Sunday. That would do. She put water on for tea when the phone rang again.

"Alice?"

"Hello, Leighton." It seemed funny to address him by a name that sounded as if it should be his surname, not his first. "I got your message."

"And?"

"I think it would be wonderful. How did you know I liked the Pops?"

"I didn't, but it just occurred to me that we might like the same kind of music—the mellow kind you can hum along with. I don't care for what my boys listen to."

"My thoughts exactly."

"Should I go casual or dress up?" he asked now. "Seems I don't have much choice between a suit and Levis."

"Well, I hear from Courtney that anything goes. I'd say casual."

"Good."

"And I have just the outfit to wear," Alice added.

Alice had a skirt in mind. It was a flowered challis and hit her midcalf. She'd wear a solid pink top and jacket. She loved challis. The material was soft and made her feel young—not that she'd been thinking about feeling young lately. Her heart was doing strange flip-flops. What was wrong with her? This was a casual acquaintance. One didn't get all excited over friends, now, did they?

Her hands ran through her short hair. Well, there wasn't much to do with her hair. One style and that was it. That was probably good. "Lord, You sure dish up surprises. A date for tonight and a grandchild on the horizon. Not sure I can stand so much excitement.

"And, Lord, I sure hope I know what I'm doing. I don't want anything serious to happen, so is it wrong to look forward to going out with this man? Is this part of Your plan for me?"

As Alice looked in the mirror at her flushed face, she thought of Carl. It was as if he were smiling, urging her on. It had been a long time since she'd felt a man's arm on her shoulder or held hands. It looked like that was all about to change.

three

After talking to Leighton, Alice decided on a lingering bath with lavender-scented bubbles. It had been a long time since she'd taken the time for such luxury, and she intended to enjoy every minute.

Leaning back, she let the day's happenings go through her mind. It had started out as a typical early summer day at work. She was happy for the job. It got her going each day. She now had something to look forward to. Not that she didn't see Courtney and Steven, the main focus of her existence, but it wasn't the same with Courtney out and safely ensconced in her own apartment.

"You have an adjustment to make," Agnes, her dominating sister, said one Sunday a few weeks after the wedding. "You aren't the center of Courtney's universe these days."

It was true, though Alice did not consider herself to be an overbearing parent or a demanding one. And she knew from talking to other mothers that once a child was married, they lost contact. That wasn't going to happen to her. Not ever.

She reached for a towel. At times her loneliness was overwhelming, almost more than she could bear. It was at these times that she turned to a few of her memorized Bible verses. She knew she would never be alone. God was there to sustain her.

A man in her life? Alice didn't think so. That would be too big of an adjustment. Besides, this man did not live in Portland and to move elsewhere was quite impossible.

The phone rang as Alice started to dry her hair. She grabbed it before the answering machine went on.

"Alice? I know this sounds ridiculous, but do you have plans for dinner?"

"I. . . Well, there's a piece of chicken left over from Sunday."

"Why don't I stop by early and we'll go to Jake's? My son said it's one of the best places around for seafood."

"Your son's right. Jake's *is* good, and I think dinner would be lovely." Alice couldn't remember the last time she'd had dinner at Jake's, and certainly it had not been with a man.

"It's settled then. Now, if you'll give me directions to your house."

"I'm out here in Parkrose. You have a bit of a drive, and the traffic is bad. Don't go the freeway. I'd take the Burnside Bridge and come east on Sandy."

She replaced the phone and checked her face in the mirror. Pink cheeks. Yes.

Courtney called when Alice had one foot in her panty hose.

"Mom?"

"Hi, Honey. How're you feeling? And what did Steven say about having a boy?"

"Steven is thrilled. Oh, Mom, he brought home this huge teddy bear. It's just darling."

"No football?"

"No, but I'm sure that's next."

"Listen, Dear, I really want to talk, but I have to get dressed in fifteen minutes. Think I can make it?"

"Fifteen minutes? Mom? This isn't water exercise night."

"I'm going out to eat and then to the Pops concert."

"Oh, did you finally talk Agnes into going to the Pops?"

"I'm going with Leighton."

There was a long pause, and Alice knew she wouldn't get off the phone before Courtney had an explanation. And even if she hurried, she wouldn't quite be ready for the now earlier dinner date.

"Mom, I can't believe this. It's almost bizarre, so unlike you."

"His son had tickets, and rather than see them go to waste, Leighton invited me. And since we're both hungry and there are so many good places to eat downtown, we're having dinner first."

"Are you sure Jeff knows him?"

"Call Jeff."

"Well, you should be able to judge character, I guess. What did you say he did for a living?"

"He's an oyster farmer from Oysterville."

"An oyster farmer?"

"Yes. That's what they call them, I've been told. They grow them and export them to San Francisco and other areas. He's just in town on business."

"Oh."

"Honey, I'll tell you all about the evening tomorrow."

Date. Imagine. She'd thought the word *date.* After hanging up, Alice felt all giddy again. She couldn't believe the feeling that raced through her. She'd never thought about going on a date, much less feeling this way about anyone. Carl had been her whole life. And their romance was tame. In fact, her best friend Todi had asked if this was really the guy she wanted to spend the rest of her life with.

"Yes, and why do you think not?" They'd stopped after the youth meeting for Cokes at their favorite hideout. Todi drove an old beat-up Chevy, and she stared out the window with the green door that didn't match the gray body.

"When I fall in love"—Todi rolled her eyes—"I want to see sparks and feel butterflies in my tummy and expect to be with him every single minute."

"You know Carl's off on that two-week program, or I *would* be with him."

"But you don't talk about him constantly and you rarely glance at your engagement ring, and—"

Alice remembered now, after all those years, of shushing Todi up, then wondering later that night in the sanctity of her bedroom if she really did love Carl, asking God if this was the right mate for her.

Maybe they had not had a whirlwind courtship, but it had

been good and solid and strong. Never wavering. She thought of a Scripture she had marked in her Bible: "Be on your guard; stand firm in the faith; be men of courage; be strong. Do everything in love."

Besides, Todi was. . .well, Todi. How many mothers would give a child that name? Todi's mother was eccentric. Todi got a car on her sixteenth birthday and passed the driving test the same day. She drove all around, and her mother never asked when she'd be home. She liked to pretend she was lost, and Alice, being gullible, believed her. Todi was crazy, doing things Alice could only dream about, but Alice loved her like a sister.

Todi. Alice picked up a silver picture frame from the dresser. Todi had the ever-present impish smile. Her hair had turned gray before she lost it. Chemo had not stopped the cancer, and Todi died at the young age of forty. Alice swallowed hard and replaced the photo. Todi had taught her how to love life and to laugh. Agnes, Alice's serious, stalwart sister, would never have ridden a motorcycle, especially not with someone she had just met. But Todi had dared Alice to do that as she jumped on behind the friend of Carl's. Together they rode up to Rocky Butte and looked out over the city, with its twinkling lights.

Alice wondered how she could have done that, been so trusting with a man she had skated with twice. Yet she had put her trust in the man with the dark eyes, just as she was putting her trust in another man three decades later. A man with a trusting smile and a winning way. She had never told Agnes about the motorcycle ride, just as she wasn't about to tell her about tonight and her date with Leighton.

Alice and Carl had had a good marriage. They'd traveled while he was in the air force, then come back to Portland to settle down. The Cape Cod was the first house they looked at, the perfect neighborhood for the family they'd have. Except the babies didn't come. After endless prayers, Courtney was a wonderful gift from a woman who could not keep her baby.

Alice brushed a tear aside and slipped her outfit on, then the flats. She liked casual.

Had she ever thought of finding someone else? Not really. She was happy with things the way they were, happy to bask in Courtney's romance and now the expected baby. She didn't need to focus on a man. Did she?

The outfit fit her curves well. She looked sideways in the mirror. The water exercise classes had firmed her muscles, made her slim. But the most wonderful gift was the energy she had. And working for Steven had made her energy even more boundless.

Alice was applying a makeup pencil at her left eyebrow when she heard the car in the drive. One thing she'd always liked about this house was that she could hear someone coming down the driveway. She quickly penciled the other eyebrow, deciding the lipstick and blush could wait until she'd answered the door.

Leighton didn't get out of the car. Alice looked out the bedroom window and saw him sitting, waiting. He was early. Maybe he was the type that didn't like to be early and would wait until it was six.

She quickly added a touch of pink gloss and a bit of blush to her cheeks. She was ready now. If he didn't come to the door in a minute, she'd go out.

The bell rang just as her hand touched the knob.

She opened the door and smiled. He was breathtakingly handsome in the Levis and a buff-colored sports jacket. His hair was salt and pepper with a neat, trim cut but long sideburns. His eyes, a deep brown, looked at her with an almost little-boy look. Their gaze met and held.

"Alice." He stepped forward and took her hand. "You look absolutely beautiful, and I'm so glad I thought of dinner."

She took her eyes away long enough to motion him in. "We could have a cup of coffee or something, but perhaps we should get going. Jake's can be crowded, even on a weeknight."

His hand lingered on her shoulder as he helped her with

her wrap. Why did she feel so tingly? She was simply having dinner with the man.

"I think what we're doing is absolutely mad."

She looked up and saw he was serious. "Mad?"

"My asking you out, not to count the way I am feeling right now as I look at you. Alice, I haven't thought of a woman in so long. I'm totally out of practice. I don't know what to do or say. I'll be inept. You'll laugh at me."

Alice laughed then. Well, he'd given her permission, had he not?

"See?"

"I was thinking the very same thing just before you arrived. As I was dressing for this occasion, my daughter called. She thinks I'm behaving like a teenager, and quite frankly, I believe I am, too. If only my best friend Todi were here, I'd ask her what she thought."

"Todi?"

Alice smiled. "We were inseparable all through high school. And she said I didn't love my first husband madly enough."

"And did you?"

"I loved him, I guess." Alice didn't go on to add that she had never felt this way, so vulnerable, so wanting him to kiss her that she had to shake her head to make the thought go away.

"I was mad about my first wife, but she didn't feel the same. Or maybe she did at one time. I'll never know now." He glanced at his watch. "We'd better go or we'll be late for dinner and the concert."

They walked side by side up the walk, and he opened the car door. Alice swallowed again, wondering if Todi could see her from her vantage point in heaven.

The car was nice. Clean. As Alice stole a sideways glance at Leighton, liking his strong profile, she sensed this would be the first of many such dates.

four

They were early, but Jake's had a long line of patrons waiting.

"Maybe we better go somewhere else," Leighton suggested. "I don't like rushing through dinner." He wondered if she felt that way, too. Apparently she did, as she immediately turned and walked back toward his car.

"I agree. If we have to wait thirty minutes, we could be late for the concert. Let's go down on the river." Alice smiled. "I know this new place, and it just might be that everyone hasn't caught on to it yet."

Alice directed Leighton down Burnside, then south on the Naito Parkway that went along the river. Another turn and they pulled into a parking lot. The river was busy with boats and barges, and a gentle wind blew, sending Alice's hair flying. She directed Leighton down a flight of wooden steps that would take them to the floating restaurant.

"This is wonderful," Leighton said, taking her arm and helping her down the steep steps.

"I've been here just once. The seafood is terrific, and it's fun to watch the activity on the water."

"We don't have a floating restaurant at home. Can't do that with a change in the tide twice a day, but you'd like some of the places we do have. One of my favorites is on the bay. The Ark has a great menu."

Alice was delighted she had picked a place Leighton obviously enjoyed. Not everyone liked dining right on the Willamette River. The Newport Bay was well moored and moved very little, even when a barge went by and caused high waves to lap at the base of the restaurant. A man on a jet ski rode by, waving at the people on the deck.

Leighton's dark eyes met hers. "I'm glad you thought of

this place. I'll have to see if John's come here yet. I love the water and the action on it."

Alice smiled, remembering a time when her husband had bought a boat. It had been used mostly for cruising up and down the river in the summer. Courtney had learned to water-ski, and for that they often went to one of many lakes in the area. Those relaxing summer days brought back many pleasant memories.

"Did you ever water-ski?" Alice asked.

"No, have you?"

"Yes, I learned how one summer, and we skied several years until Carl sold the boat."

"I suppose I'm too old to try it now."

"Well, I sure wouldn't want to try again. Probably wouldn't be able to walk for a week," Alice said, as they both burst into laughter.

"Do you realize how nice it is here with both the Willamette and Columbia Rivers?" Leighton asked. "Not to mention Mount Hood in the distance."

Alice nodded and sipped on her root beer. "But aren't you surrounded by water on the peninsula?"

"Yes, but it's quiet on the bay. A few crabbing boats and a canoe now and then. That's about it. I'd like you to see it sometime." He forked a shrimp out of the cocktail sauce. "I've wondered about living in the mountains, but I'm not sure what I'd do there. Oystering is pretty much in my soul."

Alice wanted to say something charming and witty but knew she didn't have to worry with Leighton. It was a safe, comfortable feeling, so uncanny, since she didn't even know the man. She was attracted to him, just as he showed signs of being attracted to her, and she liked that very much. It was a good, yet exhilarating, feeling.

"What are you thinking about?" Leighton asked. "You can't smile in such a charming way and not let me know what you're smiling about."

Alice decided to tell him the truth. Why not? They weren't

kids anymore. She set her fork down. "It's just that I feel as if I've known you forever, and it's strange."

He grinned. "I tend to affect a lot of women that way."

It was a joke, she knew. His eyes gave him away with a twinkle of merriment. "Obviously, you say that to all the women you date; is that what you mean?"

"Yep, you've got my number." He turned serious then. "I've had few dates since Nancy's death. It was such a disaster, I swore off dating and just took care of my family and my business the best I knew how. But there is a woman I sort of thought about dating."

Alice wanted to ask more about this woman, but decided it wasn't any of her business. She leaned forward. "Your business sounds pretty successful."

"It's been working so far."

The waitress arrived with large bowls of clam chowder, which Leighton said he could never get enough of. "I like trying chowder everywhere I go. I have my favorite spot back home, which I can't wait to take you to. There's a gorgeous view of the ocean, and it has its beauty and charm just as your river does here."

They paused for a short blessing, each saying their own. Alice felt even more impressed by this tall, homespun man she'd barely met.

They lingered over dinner, Alice taking time with the lobster, dipping each bite in drawn butter. Leighton seemed amused until he glanced at his watch.

"Isn't the concert at eight thirty?"

"Yes. Surely it isn't that late."

"No, but we'd better go, though I know it's just a few blocks away."

Concerts were held downtown in a complex of entertainment theaters and concert halls. They arrived just as the lights dimmed.

The first song, in honor of the Fourth of July, was George M. Cohan's "Yankee Doodle Dandy." Everyone stood, cheering.

Men saluted the huge flag on stage. Alice and Leighton covered their hearts to show respect.

"I was too young for World War II or the Korean Conflict, but I joined the ROTC in high school," Leighton said.

Alice felt the warmth of his hand covering hers, as a trio ran out on the stage and sang "Don't Sit Under the Apple Tree." Alice hummed along, then stopped as she realized her voice was carrying. Leighton leaned over. "You can hum in my ear any old time you want to. I don't mind at all. In fact, I'd join you, but I would scare everyone out."

Alice wished the concert would never end. She couldn't remember the last time she'd enjoyed anything so much.

It was after ten when their clapping brought the performers out for a second encore.

Leighton insisted they go for desserts at a place his son had told him about. "John said I wasn't to miss it. That it was definitely a must."

"I'm still full," Alice protested, but seeing the firm look on his face, she gave in. It was a way to make the evening continue.

"We can split one, then," he said.

The restaurant was cozy and great for intimate dining. They settled in a back booth and ordered two black coffees and a thick slice of lemon soufflé pie with two forks.

"Alice, I find myself wishing I didn't need to return to Oysterville. I want to stay, want to take you out again, want to—" He paused. "I guess what I'm trying to say is I enjoyed the evening and hope you did, too."

She felt her heart beating faster, keeping time with the thoughts in her mind. How could this be happening? How could she be feeling this way? It made no sense. Here she'd been going along in life, thanking God every day for her many blessings, and was He now telling her there was more that He wanted her to have?

"You're not saying anything." Leighton leaned over and touched her hand. "I hope I haven't said too much. I tend to level with everyone right off. The kids always know where they stand with me."

"Quite the contrary. It's been wonderful, and I was just thinking the other day I couldn't have anything more wonderful happen. Now this."

They left the restaurant and strolled down past Pioneer Square, where another couple walked, seemingly oblivious to everyone. A full moon shone down from a dark sky. Leighton took Alice's hand as they climbed the steps toward the street where the car was parked.

"Everything looks so different at night," Alice said. "I haven't been downtown this late since forever."

She wanted the moment to last, but knew it would in her mind and heart.

"I suppose I better take you home, though I don't really want to."

"Nor do I want to go."

"We have to be careful. I feel like a teenager who can't be left alone with you for more than a minute."

They laughed at that thought as they got into the car and Leighton headed back across the river. Lights danced on the water, and the Morrison Bridge dazzled them with the pink and blue lights.

"I love the city at night," Alice said. "I like it where I live, but there's just something magical about being downtown at night."

She'd thought once of having an apartment in the downtown area, but it hadn't seemed practical. Besides, she liked the Cape Cod in Parkrose. There were memories there. Space. And love. Lots of love and laughter echoed from the rooms. How could she ever leave a place she loved so much?

"You're a happy person," Leighton said as he pulled into her driveway. "You have no idea how much that means to me."

"Your wife wasn't happy?" After saying it, she wished she could take the words back, certain that Leighton would not want to talk about the past.

He looked away. "Nancy wanted things she couldn't have. It didn't matter what I did; it was wrong. God knows I tried."

Alice touched his arm. "I'm sure you did, Leighton. Some people can't be happy. I like the old saying of Abraham Lincoln's: " 'Most people are about as happy as they make up their minds to be.' "

"For years I blamed myself for the breakup of my marriage and home. And later, when Nancy, when she ended it all, I took on more guilt. How can someone ever know another's agony?"

"I'm glad you told me. Being the typical curious female, I would have wondered about it. I'm sorry she took her life. That must have been hard on your children."

"They hadn't seen her much those last few years. Luke took it hard, though."

"And so here you are now, and you're probably wondering why."

He leaned over and kissed her forehead. "I know why I'm here and I believe God led me to you. And now I better go before I kiss you again and you find yourself inviting me in."

Long after he left, Alice stood by the window looking out into the dark night. The entire evening was like a dream. The food had been great, though she hadn't been able to eat much. The concert was lighthearted, and they'd laughed a lot. And later the dessert and stroll had ended the night.

It was midnight. She hadn't been up this late for years. And the funny thing was, she couldn't call Courtney and tell her about it. Oh, for a good friend like Todi. She'd just have to write it in her journal for posterity. And she'd always remember this one night of fun and feeling like she was loved and desired.

Leighton had said he would return soon. In the meantime, he wanted her to plan on a visit to the peninsula and to his Oysterville. Could she do that? Should she?

Yes, she would go. She wanted to go. And as she turned and saw the blinking light of the answering machine, she wondered how long ago Courtney had called.

"Mom, you should be back by now. It's eleven thirty. I checked and the concert was over at ten thirty. Where are you? I'm worried."

Alice laughed as she kicked her shoes off. Funny how the tables could turn. Here her child was worried about her, as if she were a little kid. Maybe she'd better call. If she didn't, Courtney might call the police and report a "missing mom."

She laughed again as she reached for the phone.

five

Leighton met Alice at the library the next afternoon. He had offered to pick her up, but she'd said it was quicker to ride the Max in. She had another place picked out.

"It's a quaint place on Broadway. One of my favorites." She smiled. "It has great fish and chips and a nice salad bar."

He took her hand, and she leaned into him as they walked down a few blocks. The sun had finally decided to shine after a morning of an overcast sky.

"Do you realize it would take a month of having lunch to hit all the good spots?"

He grinned. "Sounds good to me. You have more to choose from than I do at home."

Alice didn't want to ask but had to know. "Are you going back today?"

"Yes, after my appointment. I'll go to John's and pack my few things and get out of town before rush-hour traffic."

"I suppose all this traffic seems strange to you." Alice sipped her soda.

"This is true. I can go to the four-way stop in Ocean Park and if there's a car ahead of me, that's news."

After a trip to the salad bar and splitting an order of fish and chips, Leighton glanced at his watch. "My stars, how did it get so late? I have thirty minutes to make it to the northwest side of town."

"You'll make it. Relax."

"I like being early, though."

"You should be."

Not that Alice was late for appointments, but she'd learned it rarely did good to be early, since it seemed she always had to wait.

When Leighton signaled the waitress for the tab, Alice offered to leave a tip.

"Don't even think about it. It was my idea. My treat." As he walked her to the Max stop, he said, "I'll call you."

"Let me know when you get home. And I hope the restaurant places a big order."

His last glimpse was of her waving from the back of the train as it headed east.

&a

The owner was most cordial and open to Leighton's new products.

"People eat out, enjoy a dinner of oysters. They want to take something home. It could be a memento of their trip, or for local patrons, it might be something to eat later, to extend their pleasant evening."

"Yes, I know what you mean." The young man, a Mr. Nelson, younger than Leighton's sons, leaned forward. "The Original Taco House has their salad dressing and salsa for sale in a showcase just inside the door. I understand they sell a lot of both items." He nodded. "I'll take a case each of smoked and plain oysters and a dozen of the spices. I doubt that they sell as fast as the oyster products."

Leighton stood, and the two men shook hands. "I'll see that it's delivered within the week."

Leighton could have Ken, his deliveryman, bring the orders in, but he just might deliver the products himself. It would be a first, to be sure. He didn't come to Portland often. Usually, he couldn't wait to leave the traffic noises, the sound of sirens, loud boom boxes, the general sound of people rushing. He missed the quiet peninsula where people did things in their own good time. Each day when he picked up his mail, he chatted with Casey, the postmaster. He knew everyone at the store. He was friendly to the tourists who frequented his small business. They were used to instant gratification, and he didn't act as if it was an affront to wait on them, as some merchants did.

"Dad, you're semiretired," John said every time Leighton

came to town. "You have a crew working for you. What's your hurry?"

Leighton always came up with the same answer. "Son, when you're away, the boys will play. I need to stay on top of things. You know how I feel about that."

It was true. Just as every household needed a boss, an authority figure, a business needed the owner present. But it was also because Leighton had to get away. It hadn't changed in the ten years he'd been coming in on business. Until now. And all because of Alice. She made him realize he *liked* having someone there. Someone to talk to. It was a good, yet uncertain, feeling.

He hurried back and changed from his suit to casual wear for the trip home, then packed his toiletries. He stood at the window of the high-rise, looking once more out across the Willamette River. On a clear day, Mount Hood was visible fifty miles away. Hood. He'd wondered what it'd be like to ski on those runs, or to snowboard, which was the current rage. Not that he kept current. If he did, he'd be in-line skating down the sidewalk. In his day, it had been roller skates, and every Friday night he and Nancy had gone to the skating rink at the camp in Ocean Park.

Change that thought. Now you not only have to watch out for roller blades, but skateboards, too. He had been nearly mowed down by one the day he arrived.

Once outside, he looked at the sky. Rain clouds. Soon the mountain would disappear from sight. It rained in Portland a lot. It rained in Oysterville a lot. Even in June it rained. And December, January, and February. Leighton was used to it. While elsewhere people shoveled their walks in winter, people here wore raincoats, rain hats, and carried umbrellas.

His car was on the blue level of the parking garage. He paused in the entrance and thought about going back inside and calling Alice to tell her about the big order, to say he would miss her. Tell her he missed her already. But he was too old for love. Leave it to the young kids to find their one true love. Leighton would bask in his work, his four grandchildren, and his sons.

Leighton got as far as the approach to the Morrison Bridge and turned abruptly on Third Avenue. There must be a pay phone booth nearby. Most large towns had phone booths on every corner. Then he spotted one. He'd have to park in a zone with a parking meter, but he had change. He always carried change. Yes, a cell phone would have been nice about now, and he could hear John lamenting, "You have a laptop, Dad, but won't get a cellular phone. What if something happens on the road?"

So far nothing had.

He dug out Alice's phone number and dialed, hoping she'd be there. If she'd stayed downtown, they could have taken a drive, stopped for coffee somewhere, or just walked in the City Park Blocks. It was his favorite place in the downtown area.

"Leighton? I thought you'd be long gone by now."

Did he catch a hint of surprise? Delight in her voice? He swallowed, not wanting to sound ridiculous, wondering what she might say.

"I'm heading out and just wanted to say good-bye again." It sounded inane, but he felt compelled, felt as if God was pushing him that way.

"How did the appointment go?"

"The Ringside placed the largest order so far."

"Leighton, that's wonderful! How encouraging."

He had a sudden irrepressible urge to touch her, to hear her laugh. "I'm going to miss you." The words were out and he couldn't snatch them back.

"I'm going to miss you, too."

He could visualize her soft blue eyes, the funny little half grin she did a lot, and wondered at the thump, thumping of his heart. "It's crazy, isn't it?" he said. "Us two oldsters acting like a couple of kids. I hope you know this is so unusual for me."

She laughed and the sound warmed his heart. "And unusual for me," she murmured. "Yes, crazy but nice. Courtney thinks I've lost my mind."

"I'll call you when I get to Oysterville." The noise from

the traffic made it hard to hear, and besides, someone was waiting for the booth.

"Good-bye—oh—and Leighton, next time you come to Portland, I want you over for dinner."

"I'll count on it."

He replaced the receiver. He'd wanted to say more than good-bye, but what? He stepped out of the booth, put the slip of paper in his pocket, and headed back to his car. Man, but her voice sounded good!

He'd be thinking about their times together, dreaming of when he'd see her again, thanking God for giving him hope, for making his heart light again. And now he had a dinner to look forward to.

&

Soon Leighton was out of the traffic and winging his way west. He stuck in his favorite tape, *Fiddler on the Roof,* as he drove over the familiar miles to the peninsula. He had the songs memorized. The boys laughed at him, though he remembered when they were young and he put the tape in, they'd sing along. Especially Aaron.

He hadn't told Alice about Aaron, why he'd run away, the problems they had. Didn't most families have problems? Kids ran off all the time, and Leighton figured when Aaron was ready to come home, he would. There wasn't much Leighton could do about it. Once in a while Luke or Tom mentioned their brother. Cora brought his name up often.

His thoughts went to home and Cora. She hadn't crossed his mind until now. She'd be at his house, have it all clean and shiny, and dinner in the oven. She had loved Aaron, but that's because she'd taken care of him when he was young, after Aunt Rita died. If the truth were known, Cora spoiled Aaron. She'd also been good with Hannah and had suggested once that perhaps Aaron left because he couldn't stay and watch his sister die.

"Hannah may live for a good many years," Leighton had argued. "Nobody knows how long she has."

Cora shook her head. "Leighton, the child is dying. Right

before our eyes. Don't pretend when pretending is no good. You're only fooling yourself."

She'd been partly wrong and he was partly right. Though she grew weaker and could do less, not even walk down the road to pick up the daily paper, Hannah had lived two more years.

He thought again of Aaron, as he sang, "If I were a rich man." Aaron, eyes wide and innocent, had asked, "But, Daddy, aren't we rich?"

He had leaned over, ruffling the child's sandy blond hair. "We're certainly not rich, but we're not poor, either."

Had he not given him enough attention? With worry over Hannah and her taking so much of his time, Aaron had been ignored more than the older boys. Leighton hadn't meant to ignore him. God knew how much he loved him, just as he loved all his children.

As for Nancy, she kept everything inside her. Unable to voice her feelings about how she felt, she had not leaned on God for help, nor had she sought help from a doctor. The boys had come along, one every two years. She'd been a good mother. A caring mother. Yet he had failed her. He had not given her enough attention. It seemed that his love and attention was showered on his sons from the time they were toddlers right until they went off to school. Then Hannah was born, and Nancy cried all the way home from Portland after they'd seen a specialist, loud sobs that tore at Leighton and made him want to stop the car, pull her into his arms, and tell her it would be all right.

"We can handle this, Honey," he'd said instead, looking over at his young, distraught wife.

"I wanted a perfect child. All our other children are perfect."

"God knew we would love her anyway and take extra-special care of her."

"I don't want that responsibility."

As if on cue, Hannah woke from her car seat in the back. Whimpering, she waited for her mother's arms, but Nancy didn't budge.

"Do you think she's hungry?" Leighton asked. "I could

pull over so you could nurse her."

"And then watch while she throws up everything?"

"Oh, Honey, don't be like this."

She hadn't faced him the day she left, but he found a note on the dining room table.

Please forgive me for being weak. I know you will find someone to help with Hannah, someone who can hold her and give her the love and attention she needs. That person just isn't me.

"But what about our sons?" Leighton had said to the still, empty room. "What about Luke, John, Thomas, and Aaron? They need a mother. And I need a wife." He'd anguished long into the night, unable to sleep. The thought came to mind that God didn't want him to fear, that He wouldn't give him a larger burden than he could bear.

He had blamed himself, though friends and family said he'd done everything he could. Yet he knew he had not.

When Cora moved up to Oysterville and offered to keep house and cook and mother the Walker children, Leighton had seen her as an answer to prayer.

Cora was indeed a godsend. She loved horses and the outdoors, and the boys took to her right off. She didn't seem to mind caring for a child who coughed constantly and needed to be pounded. She loved to cook, and he'd often find freshly baked cookies when he returned from the cannery. Always there was a pot of stew or chowder or a roast in the oven. Leighton knew he couldn't have survived without her.

Cora had a big heart, and once he sensed she cared for him in that way, but he didn't look at women or think about marrying again. He just couldn't.

He wondered if Cora would be there as he stopped and picked up his mail. Often she was gone when he got home from work, but it might be different today. She would want to know how the trip went and if he'd sold anyone on his new products.

Her car was parked in the usual spot under the trees.

six

Leighton's heart sank. He'd expected Cora to be here, yet he wasn't prepared for what he needed to say. He liked having her here. He had always known she wanted more, but though he was fond of her, he hadn't made any moves. And now after meeting Alice, it was as if a whole new world had opened up. He couldn't quite explain it, but he knew he wanted to see Alice again. Somehow he needed to convey this to Cora.

He didn't have a chance to retrieve the spare key from under the hedgehog foot scraper before the door flew open. Cora, hair pulled back with a dark green ribbon, smiled expectantly.

"So? How did it go? Did you sell the oysters? I thought you were *never* going to get here. I made dinner hours ago—" She paused, her eyes meeting his level gaze. "I suppose you stopped at Hump's or somewhere on the Oregon side."

"It went better than I expected." He tossed his jacket over a chair. "Everyone I met was receptive to the idea and placed an order."

"But that's wonderful!" Her eyes shone. "You don't seem too excited about it."

"Just tired."

"Of course. Come on and let me heat you up some dinner."

He moved past her, wondering how to broach the subject. He never had been one to mince his thoughts. Besides, Cora knew him well. She understood his moods, his concerns for his family, the business. She was special, but he couldn't think of her in a romantic way.

"Is something wrong?" She leaned over and smoothed dark hair back from his forehead.

He moved. "Cora, I don't feel like talking tonight."

"I understand. I'm far too chatty at times. It's my worst fault." She grabbed a hanger out of the hall closet.

Groaning, he knew this would be far worse than he'd ever anticipated.

"I had a problem with the laptop and had someone look at it."

"Is it fixed?" She looked at the small case that held the computer. She'd thought it was a frivolous expense at the time and had told him so.

"It's fine now. It wasn't serious."

"Then you should be feeling good about everything." She looked at him expectantly.

I am, oh, I am, but how can I tell her?

"I cleaned out the refrigerator. It was getting pretty gross."

"Thanks. I appreciate it."

"Leight, you're acting kinda weird. Is John okay? Have I done something?"

"John's fine. Portland's fine. The car runs fine. I'm fine. It's just that, well, when I took the computer in, this woman was there and we had lunch today."

Her eyes narrowed. "You mean—" Her voice fell. He turned and gently held her shoulders.

"I wasn't looking for anyone; you know that. I told you years ago when Nancy first left that I would never love anyone again."

"But now it's suddenly different?"

He shook his head, knowing he'd said too much, had hurt this woman whom he knew had strong feelings for him. "Things happen, you know, things you can't explain. Things just sort of clicked."

He thought Cora would say something, but she stood, staring out the window at the bay, her voice barely audible when she did speak.

"I've waited for you, Leighton. I thought that someday you might grow to love me. I know your likes and dislikes. I could run the business, if need be. The boys respect me. I. . .

What went wrong? I can see that loving you was a mistake."

"It's never a mistake to love someone, is it? And I can never repay you for helping with Hannah and the boys and the cooking and cleaning. You did far more than I ever paid you for. And you're such a wonderful friend." He wanted to continue, but her voice cut through him.

"Friend? That's all this has been? Just friendship?"

"Oh, Cora, I never promised you anything, did I?"

She sat on the small love seat that looked out over the bay, staring into space, as if watching the trees that swayed in the gentle breeze.

He had hurt her deeply. He had always been afraid he would hurt her in the end. How could he not, when he didn't feel the same for her?

"I should have let you go," he finally said. "You needed to find someone to love, to marry, to have a child with."

"I couldn't, Leighton. Not feeling the way I do." She raised her face to his, the hint of tears in her blue eyes. "I could never, ever give you up. It's that simple."

She rose and walked to the other end of the living room, her hands touching the keys of the old upright. "What's she like, Leighton? Is she young? Beautiful? *Charming?*"

He slumped into one of the old easy chairs that filled one corner of the large room. "I can't even describe her to you. It's strange, I know. She has a lilt to her voice. Doesn't that beat all? The one thing I keep thinking about is her voice and how it sounds."

He also remembered that she was tall, her figure was rounded, and she had brown hair. Her eyes were blue, but he wasn't even positive about that. But when she talked, he had listened. And her words, the expression, the inflection in her voice had captured his attention.

"You fell in love with a *voice?* I find that difficult to believe. And what does she think about you? You've said how you feel about her but nothing about her feelings."

He didn't want to have this discussion now. Of course, he

never wanted or liked discussions. Especially not with a strong-willed woman like Cora. She seemed to read things that weren't there or to hear something he hadn't said.

The room was dark now, as it often was on cloudy days. She stood at the piano but did not play. She was a good pianist and often played songs she knew he liked, but she only touched the old, polished wood. He should never have led her on. He hadn't really; she had led herself on.

"Is she coming here to visit?"

"I don't know."

"You didn't ask her?"

He sighed. "As a matter of fact, it was mentioned, but I doubt that she would come right now. Her daughter is expecting her first baby, and Alice has just the one child. She probably wouldn't leave her now. It's far more likely that I'll go back to Portland."

"How old is she? And I suppose she's thin." Cora had been so sure if Leighton had ever found someone, it would be a younger, more alluring woman. She, for all her good points, had bad ones, the main one being her weight. She had tried diets, a hundred or so, but nothing ever worked.

Leighton turned the small reading lamp on beside his chair. "I don't know her age, but she's definitely older. Courtney is twenty-four or so."

"You met her daughter and all her family?"

"Just the daughter. It's her husband who owns the computer business, and Alice works part-time for him."

"Alice," Cora said with a sneer.

"You'd like her. She's quite personable."

"I just bet." Cora reached over and grabbed her purse. "I am not giving up, Leighton. I waited this long and will wait longer. She won't want to move here. Just you wait and see."

Before he could answer, she'd turned and gone out the front door, slamming it behind her.

Her words stunned him. He had not wanted to talk about Alice. His feelings were so new, so unexpected; he didn't know what he felt or what she felt. Cora had been a friend all these years. If something was going to happen between them, wouldn't it have happened already? How could he make himself feel something that was not there? Would she want someone who did not love her in return? Somehow he could not believe that.

Cora had been engaged once and moved to Cathlamet, a small town on the Columbia River. No one had been more surprised than he was when she came back home to Oysterville. She changed jobs from teaching English to running a bed and breakfast. Then she came to care for his family when Aunt Rita died.

He hadn't meant to hurt her. It wasn't his way. He should have known what was happening long before this. After the boys were gone and Hannah had died, why had Cora stayed on? Had he asked her to? Funny, but he couldn't even remember now.

Leighton sat a while longer, his mind moving forward. Tomorrow he'd check with Luke, see how things had been in his absence. Luke was essentially the boss, hiring and firing, keeping track of production numbers, making sure everything was in working order. Leighton was a figurehead more than anything. He'd put in a good many hours in the field and in the cannery. It had been hard with Hannah so sick. He'd taken off early to relieve Aunt Rita in the earlier days, as a baby needed constant attention, and it was too much for just one person.

In the morning he'd make out the new orders, adding the restaurants to his database. For now, he needed to call Alice and let her know he had arrived home.

≥

The day after Leighton left, Alice called Steven.

"I want a modem so I can get E-mail." Leighton had told her last night that his son was installing the program, and he would be able to write to her every day, maybe even twice.

"Alice, I asked a couple of months ago if you wanted to go

on the Internet and you said no."

"Changed my mind."

"This guy you met doesn't have anything to do with that, does it?"

"A person can change their mind, yes?"

"I'll do it on Sunday. Can't get to it before that."

"Sunday's fine."

☙

Steven was there when Courtney and Alice returned from Gresham and the customary visit and lunch with Agnes.

"How's it going?" Alice asked. "I'm so eager to use it. You'll leave the directions, right? I tend to forget things."

"Yes, of course. It's installed. I'll show you in a minute." He pulled Courtney close, nibbling the back of her neck.

"I have this tape I want to watch," Courtney said. "It's about natural childbirth."

"In a sec, okay, Hon? I need to show your mother how to bring up her mail."

They walked back to the office, and Steven handed Alice a slip of paper with her password. "Don't tell anyone the password. And here's your address. You can change it, if you want."

"I'm Alyce?" She stared at the paper.

"Your name was already taken, so you have to choose another spelling. Sorry. Now you are *Alyce@pdx.com*. Be sure you don't put a period after the com, though, okay?"

Alice nodded as she brought up an empty document. "Just a minute." She looked in her letter file for Leighton's E-mail address.

"Why don't you send a card?"

"A card?"

"Yes. Some web sites offer free electronic cards. They have music, too. And there's all sorts of categories."

Alice nodded. "That would be fun."

After sending a *Just thinking of you and here's my address* card, Steven showed her how to log off the Internet. "You want the line to be free for phone calls."

As if on cue, the phone rang and Alice grabbed the extension.

"Leighton! I just sent my first E-mail message." She giggled.

"Hey, great. I'll send one back. Talk to you on-line soon."

"Wait. Are you still coming next Thursday?"

"Yes."

"I'm thinking about you," she said.

"And me, you."

"I have to go. Courtney's yelling from the living room."

"Mom?" Courtney bolted up and shut off the VCR. "Was that Leighton on the phone?"

Her face felt flushed. "Well, yes."

"And he's the reason you got on-line."

"Yes. E-mail is going to be fun and a lot cheaper than the telephone."

"Okay, let's look at the tape." Steven pushed the start button. Courtney lay flat on her back, her hands placed on the small mound that was the growing baby. Steven nodded. "We may as well practice now. See how it works."

The tape showed various exercises and ways to breathe. Steven leaned over, breathing along with her.

"Seems you don't need that quite yet," Alice said.

"You're right!" Courtney rolled to a sitting position. "Mom, I'm worried about you. You can't be serious about getting involved at this time in your—" She stopped, as if knowing she'd stepped over the bounds.

"At this time in my life? Was that what you were going to say?" Alice walked past her daughter and into the kitchen, where she put the water on for tea.

"Oh, Mom, I didn't mean it the way it sounded." Courtney was at her side, hand touching her shoulder. "It's just that I worry about you. I'd hate to see you get hurt."

Steven stood in the doorway, his lanky form filling the space. "Courtney has a point, but I also think your mom isn't the type to go off half-cocked with some guy she hardly knows."

"Exactly!" Alice turned, tea bag in hand. "I find Leighton

attractive. He's nice. Attentive. All things I'd forgotten about since your father died."

"But Daddy was your whole life."

"And life is for the living, seems I remember hearing once," Steven said. "I think you should see this man. I know John, and if his dad's even half as nice, you can't go wrong."

"But, Steven," Courtney implored, rolling her eyes, "he lives at the coast. How can Mother even think of letting this go any further?"

Alice turned the water off and got out her favorite ceramic cup, a colorful red, green, blue, and yellow one that her sister, Agnes, had made years ago in a ceramics class. She dipped the bag up and down more times than usual, willing herself to say the right words, if she, indeed, needed to comment at all.

"He seems very nice, and that's all I'm saying about it." Steven left the room, while Courtney, never backing down from a discussion of any sort, put her hands on her hips.

"Mom, you don't know a thing about him. Is he a believer?"

"As a matter of fact, he is." Alice hummed as she dumped a teaspoon of sugar into her cup and stirred.

"Mother! You don't use sugar in your tea."

Alice just smiled.

"I cannot believe this person has affected you this way."

Alice rummaged around for something to go with the tea, but could only find saltines. She wasn't in the mood for crackers.

"Your father was methodical, Courtney, and I'm afraid you take after him."

"He wasn't my father, so there's no way I could 'take after him,' as you say."

Alice felt as if she'd been punched. Courtney had to be upset to come out with that statement. Because she was adopted, any traits she had were not inherited, but some she had developed over the course of years, of watching and doing by example.

"You know what I meant," Alice said. She fought off the

sudden tears that threatened. Nobody knew unless they had tried to have children how it felt, how wonderful it was when you finally could adopt, and how it was on that first day with the tiny bundle in your arms. She had never forgotten the feeling and felt thrice blessed now that Courtney would be bringing a child into the world. Soon Alice would feel that thrill all over again, even though the child wouldn't share her bloodline.

"Mom." Courtney put her arm around her mother. She had to lean up to do it since she was short and her mother stood a head higher, even in stocking feet. "I didn't mean to hurt you. I'm just concerned, that's all. Just like you were when I went to Illinois in search of my birth mother. It's okay to be concerned, isn't it?"

Alice let out a sob and turned to pull her daughter close. "Of course it's okay to be concerned." Alice dabbed at her cheeks with a tissue she'd found in her pocket. "Just don't try to be the boss."

At that, they both laughed, and Alice took her tea into the living room. Steven had rewound the tape and started it over.

"Steven, Honey, it isn't going to happen for five months," Courtney said, wrapping her arms around his neck.

He pulled her down and kissed her cheek. "I know that, Court, but I'm going to be the most ready father there ever was."

Minutes later, Alice was back in the kitchen, checking the pot roast and getting the drippings ready for gravy. Preparing the Sunday meal always brought back the memory of that first night when Steven returned to the second service and came to sit beside Courtney. Alice had known then that something was happening between the young couple, and here they all were less than a year later.

"God certainly works fast sometimes," Tina, Courtney's best friend, had said that afternoon after the wedding and they were all eating wedding cake and talking about the couple.

"Yes, He does," Alice said. "And when one follows Him completely, there's no mistaking what He's given."

Now as they sat around the table, they held hands, and Steven asked the blessing.

The meal was quieter than usual. Afterward, Alice shooed the two out of the kitchen so she could clean up. She needed time alone to think about Leighton more clearly, to wonder, to question, to marvel at the pounding of her heart at the mere thought of him. Even now she could smell the woodsy scent of his cologne.

Maybe it isn't good for man to live alone, she mused as she placed the last plate in the dishwasher. Maybe God wanted her to be with Leighton. This could be His plan for her. The big problem was in convincing Courtney that her mother just might need something else besides loving her daughter, son-in-law, and expected grandchild.

She slipped into her bedroom and looked at her flushed cheeks. It was strange, this feeling that engulfed her. Yet he did live far away. How could they possibly see each other that often? And she could never—no, absolutely never— think of moving to the coast. It would be too far from her precious family.

Yet, she dreamed of him, wanted him to think of her, wanted to see him again. How could she possibly wait four more days?

seven

In the two days since he'd come home from Portland, Leighton found his life had returned to a semistate of normalcy. But he had more bounce in his step and a reason for getting up in the mornings. He'd take his cup of coffee and the binoculars and sit in the love seat.

The bay was calm, the tide in, and the beauty of the sunrise caused his heart to swell. He'd never tired of looking out over the water to the Willapa Hills in the distance and watching while a crabber came up the bay. Crab was plentiful in the bay, but the crab pots were set out only for certain months, and the season had just begun.

God had been good to this little spot, this forgotten finger of land next to the ocean on the west, the bay on the east, and the Columbia River on the south. He loved the clean air and took a deep breath before downing his coffee and heading to work.

It wasn't even six yet, and the morning was nippy. He pulled a cap on before hopping into the truck.

Luke had left a note on the office blackboard.

Dad, I'll be late today. Lisa has an appointment with the doctor, and I said I'd go with her.

Leighton erased the note and wondered what was going on. Lisa was never sick. And if she was, she wouldn't need Luke to go with her. Unless. . .

Soon the first shipment would be brought in for sorting. Four workers would work on the line for two hours, have a short break, then work until noon. He'd go into the store, check supplies, and make sure there was enough for the weekend. Tourists were arriving in droves. If it wasn't for them, business would be slow, but he sure wished they'd learn to drive the speed limit. It was a complaint of all old-timers.

For some reason, Alice's smile flashed through his mind. Would she fit in with this operation?

Stop, he commanded himself. He didn't really know her. One dinner, a night out at the concert, followed by a lunch was not much, yet he felt comfortable around her.

The phone rang. It was Luke.

"Dad! I knew you'd be there."

"What's up? Is something wrong with Lisa?"

"No, it's just the usual."

"The usual? Could you be a bit more specific?"

"You know. It happened to you enough times."

"No, I don't know." He didn't realize he'd raised his voice until one of his workers looked over.

"We're having a baby, Dad."

"A baby? I thought you said three was enough."

"Well, things happen and there you are."

"Don't worry about rushing in. Take your time, Son. We're doing okay. No problem."

Luke started stammering. "I understand you met someone."

"You've talked with John, then."

"No. Not John. John and I never talk. You know that. It was Cora."

Cora. Of course she would be talking about it. That's the way it was here. Everyone knew everyone else's business. Cora would have people in her corner, and he'd be classified an A-1 jerk for not asking her to marry him.

"Don't believe everything you hear."

"Dad! Don't you think I know that?"

"Cora and I had words. Haven't seen her, but that's okay. Her bossiness gets to me. She doesn't own me, after all."

"Still, she thought she had a chance that someday you'd get over Mom and—"

"That's what I mean," Leighton interrupted. "I got over your mother long ago. I just don't want to risk getting hurt again."

"Is this Alice nice?"

"Luke, would I like someone who wasn't?"

"No, I suppose not. Guess I can trust your judgment."

"Thanks for the vote of confidence. Alice is a city gal. I doubt that anything will come of it." Yet he found his heart pounding at the thought of her.

"Some city gals want to be country gals."

"How's Lisa feeling?" Leighton had always been adept at changing the topic of conversation. Nancy had accused him of dodging the issue at hand more than once. And perhaps he did.

"Yucky, about now. She hopes to get something for the nausea."

"Are you two happy about the baby?"

"Yeah, Dad. Of course. Why wouldn't we be?"

Leighton let his breath out. Nancy had hated each pregnancy. He wondered now why they hadn't been more careful. Two children would have suited her better than four sons and a sick daughter.

"Just wondering."

"Lisa loves children. She's not like my mother."

Of course Luke knew about his mother. He'd been twelve the day she packed her bags and left them.

"Why don't I take you guys out to celebrate tonight? We could try that new place in Long Beach. I hear it has good food."

"Sure. I'll check with Lisa. Gotta run."

Leighton mused how the only time he had a real conversation with Luke was on the phone. They could be in the same building, outside checking lines, or sharing any number of tasks and not say more than two words. At work they were there to work. The phone was for communicating.

He couldn't help but think about Luke as he replaced the receiver. He had always been sensible. Forthright. No man could have asked for a better son. He could rely on him to make the right choices, and he seemed to have a natural business sense. He was a lucky man. Neither Tom nor John wanted anything to do with the oyster business.

And Aaron. Leighton felt deep regret about his missing son. Was Aaron happy? Was he even still alive? He had so hoped in the earlier days after Aaron ran away that he'd call and say he was on his way home. Then he hoped he'd just call to say he was all right. Was he living out of a suitcase, or had he found a good job?

Kids. And wives. Sometimes a man was lucky and got a loving wife and kids who made him proud. Nancy. Why hadn't he suspected the problem with Nancy, that she had depression? He'd thought he knew her before they married. Why hadn't her dark, dancing curls, her laughing blue gray eyes given him some small warning? He loved her so, but his love didn't matter, didn't help. It just hadn't been enough.

Leighton turned the lights on and inspected the bins where the oysters were sorted and shucked. State law required that the bins be washed with a bleach solution at the end of each day. If they had been cleaned properly, he'd smell it. He leaned over for the telltale scent.

They were fine. He went to the back and checked supplies. He'd have to make a trip across the river on Thursday. Of course, if he was that far, he could just turn the car east and keep going until he arrived in Portland.

Alice. He couldn't get her face out of his mind. Was it because it had been so long since he'd been with a woman? Could it be that God was guiding him in this direction? How did one ever know for certain? As with everything in life, there were risks. Could he risk getting his heart broken?

eight

Leighton dreaded waiting even a few more days to see Alice. It was as if he now questioned how he felt about her and wondered if she would look at him in that same way, her eyes showing interest. Being apart was not a good idea. On the downside of fifty-three, it was as if life were passing him by. As a young man he'd felt he had forever, but now he knew it wasn't true. Nobody had forever. Only through the grace of the Lord Jesus Christ did anyone have eternal life.

He also believed that one could make or break their happiness. He had broken it once and felt he wanted to try again. He *needed* to try again. He was sorry about Cora. She had stopped by once to pick up a jacket she'd left. She'd straightened the papers in the living room, clucking her tongue over the condition of the kitchen.

"You do need a woman to take care of things." She put her hands on her hips. "Why don't I just come once a week?"

"I don't think that will be necessary." He paused for a long moment, as if searching for the right words. "Cora, more than anything I'm sorry for hurting you. I hope you believe that."

She held out a small box. "Photos. I had them at my house. Just kept forgetting to give them to you."

He took the box and thanked her. "I don't remember you taking pictures."

"Yes, well—I gotta dash. See you." She left with a half wave.

Lifting the lid, Leighton saw that the pictures were scattered; no organization here, which surprised him. Cora, being so efficient, would have had them in an album. Then he saw the bits of black paper on the back. She'd taken them out of one of those old photo albums, but why hadn't she left them in there?

The box of assorted photo albums was in the hall closet. He looked on the bottom shelf, but they weren't there. A small picture was under spare blankets. It was of Nancy and him when they first married. Had Cora taken the albums, then decided she'd better return the photos? But why would she take the pictures out of the album and not return it?

He went back to the living room and sifted through the photos.

A laughing Aaron and Hannah looked back at him in the picture on top. Tears came to his eyes. His children. And he didn't know where one of them was. Hannah was in heaven, but Aaron? Where might Aaron be?

There were the boys fishing, horseback riding, a picnic up at Leadbetter Point, picking oysters, the cannery after it had been rebuilt. A photo taken at Thanksgiving and Christmas. Then he realized that none of the photos were of him. Had she kept those? But again, he wondered why. It didn't make sense.

He set the photos back and paced across the living room. Had Cora taken other things? If so, how would he know? He didn't keep track of dishes, knickknacks, or anything like that.

Cora was a needy person. She needed to be needed. He was sure of that. Not only was she intelligent, she was clever and steadfast. Loyal. She would make some man a very good wife. He just wasn't that man.

He put the photos back in the closet and wondered why Cora had taken them home. Surely that must be what happened. He'd have to ask her about it sometime.

❧

Alice was thrilled with E-mail. She checked the mailbox first thing in the morning, and there was always a letter because Leighton rose early. She answered right off, though she figured he wouldn't be home to check until that evening.

He sent crazy cards with messages. She sent cards back.

One day they'd written five times and talked on the phone once.

"Just have to hear your voice, you know," Leighton said.

"And I like hearing your voice as well."

"How's Courtney doing?"

"Just fine. I think they have the entire nursery furnished and a stack of clothes in the chest. It's her old chest that she painted a pale blue. And I've got the small downstairs bedroom turned into a nursery."

"Sounds great. My son Luke and his wife are expecting. This is the fourth for them."

"Oh, my."

"I guess we like big families."

"So do I. I would have had one more after Courtney, but the good Lord didn't look at it that way. Two possible adoptions fell through, then I just decided it was too heartbreaking to get my hopes up only to have them come crashing down."

"So now you will have grandchildren to enjoy."

ஐ

Over the next few days, Alice went through the motions of living. Courtney laughed at her inability to sit still.

"I've never seen you like this, Mom." She shook her head. "I guess it's true—the old adage that anyone at any age can fall in love."

"I never said I was in love—"

"You didn't have to."

"I know perfectly well that life will go on as before if I never see Leighton Walker again."

"It's just that he captured your heart whether you want to admit it or not."

"Maybe you're right, Sweetie. I wasn't looking. You know that. But he's so interesting and the fact that he believes in God—well, that makes him even more special."

"So you said before, and praise God for that," Courtney said. "I always said that I hoped you'd find a good Christian man, should you ever start looking for someone."

"And that's the weird part. I wasn't—"

"Looking," Courtney finished her mother's sentence. "Yes. It just happened. It's all part of God's timing. Like Steven and me. What if he hadn't come to our church that Sunday morning?"

"Exactly."

Alice poured them each another cup of tea. Courtney had quit drinking coffee in favor of herbal teas, which wouldn't hurt her baby. "I have a surprise for you," Alice said.

"A surprise?"

Alice brought a large shopping bag in and began taking out the contents. "Little undershirts. And here's two pair of shoes that you wore when you were little. And of course this yellow bunny sleeper is precious. Remember how you used to call it your bear? Your father kept saying it's a bunny, but you insisted that it was a bear."

Courtney held the clothes close. "Mom, these are so special. I'll treasure them."

Long after Courtney had left, Alice wondered what she was going to do with her hours. She simply could not sit still, and she had cleaned out the closets, put new shelf paper in the kitchen, and had filled three boxes to give to the disabled veterans' group. Should she offer to work another day in the office or volunteer more hours at the hospital? She could get involved with the literacy program. But would she be able to concentrate on anything? Her mind wandered, and the little thread of excitement that coursed through her veins was still there. She might do more harm than help.

As if in answer to her flitting mind, the phone rang. Leighton's deep voice seemed to fill the whole room.

"I'm leaving in the morning. Not much point in waiting another day. How does that sound?"

"I can have dinner ready. I'll put in my famous oven Swiss steak. It's delicious. You'll love it. I'll ask Courtney to bring a green salad, and there's a pie in the freezer made from last year's rhubarb."

"Sounds like a plan."

"Be careful, Leighton." *I couldn't bear if anything happened to you now,* she wanted to say, but didn't.

After hanging up, she immediately dialed Courtney. "I know you just got home, but how about coming for dinner tomorrow?"

"I was just there, Mom. Why didn't you ask me then?"

"Because I didn't know it then. Leighton just called and will be here at dinnertime. I really want you to get to know him, and Steven hasn't even met him."

"I'll call Steven and get back to you."

It was a done deal, and now Alice would clean and buy the beef and other ingredients. She wondered if his son was as bothered about his sudden romance as her daughter was. It seemed silly when she thought about it. Why wouldn't Courtney be happy that she'd found someone? Then she and Steven wouldn't need to worry about taking care of her in her old age.

Two trips in less than ten days. And more messages than she could count, plus phone calls. She'd say she was being pursued.

And on that happy thought, she grabbed her purse and headed out the door for the closest grocery store. She had all night to wait, and wondered what she'd find to do.

nine

It was nine o'clock before Leighton got out of Oysterville. Ken loaded the cases of oysters on the old Chevy pickup. The company owned a delivery truck, but he didn't want to take it. It was better to leave it for Luke, in case something came up.

"Dad, you're driving this into Portland today?" He scratched his head. "Why? It's far cheaper for UPS to deliver, or let Ken take it or even me." A broad grin crossed his face. "Oh. Got it! Finally came to me. I'm thick at times, you know."

Leighton hit his knee with his cap, as if there were dust to shake off. "Yeah, well, I just want to make the trip. I made another appointment at a place Alice suggested."

"If you're finding new clientele, that's a good enough reason. And guess I should have suspected that, with you wearing a white shirt and tie." He leaned over and flipped the tie with his hand. "Of course the cap's gotta go."

"How's Lisa doing? Getting over the morning sickness?"

"It isn't going to work," Luke said, rolling his eyes. "You can't change the subject on me."

"Okay, okay. I'm going in mainly to see Alice. Is that what you wanted to hear?"

"Yeah, guess it was. So when is she coming here so we can all meet her?"

"ASAP," Leighton said. Hearing raised voices inside, he pushed past his son.

Luke often hired Mexican-Americans, but the local men, who had lived on the peninsula all their lives, resented others coming in and "taking over our jobs," Olson, the spokesperson, said. Sometimes a fight developed between the two races, and Luke had to reprimand them. Just last week he had fired two troublemakers, and it looked as if he might have to do that again. It probably wasn't the best time for Leighton to leave. He'd always run a smooth operation and resented that there was more trouble these days. Some of the younger Anglo men were lazy and didn't want to work. They then picked on the "Mexies," as they called them, for making them look bad.

"Do you want me to take care of that?" Leighton asked, as the voices inside grew louder.

Luke headed for the door. "No, I'll handle it. You go on and I'll see you when you get back."

"You'll let me know if anything else comes up?"

"And how will I do that, Dad?"

Leighton held up a cell phone. "Forgot to tell you, but I bought this yesterday. Here's the number."

A smile crossed Luke's face. "I don't believe it. You finally did it. First E-mail and now a cell phone. Welcome to the twenty-first century, Dad."

Leighton gave him a high five and strode over to the truck. The last time he'd taken the car, but if they went anywhere, Alice would have to drive or settle for the ole Chevy.

As he drove down Sandridge, he passed by Nancy's parents' old house. He still got a funny feeling when he remembered the times he'd knocked at the door, shyness overtaking him. He had always kept in touch for the boys' sake. They were the only grandparents left now. He swallowed hard, wishing his parents were still alive. His mom would have liked Alice.

He made a left-hand signal to turn onto Highway 103 when a honk sounded. He looked on the opposite side and saw Cora. She honked again. He honked back. She pulled a U-turn and came up behind him, using her flashers. Was something wrong? Had Luke sent her after him? No, she was heading north. He pulled over and seconds later she hopped out.

"Where are you going with all those crates?"

"Making a delivery." He avoided her gaze, though he could feel her eyes scrutinizing him. He expected her to say something about the tie, but she didn't. She just stood with hands on hips.

"It wouldn't be to Portland, now, would it?"

"Sure is."

"I don't suppose you want company."

He couldn't believe she'd suggest it. Wouldn't that look ducky to drive up to Alice's with Cora in tow?

"I'm staying over at John's. He's just got the one spare bedroom."

"You could easily make the trip in a day."

Why is she doing this? She knows about Alice. Why act as if she doesn't? She's never before asked to go to Portland.

"Cora, I really must go. I have an appointment with a restaurant. Sorry. Maybe another time."

She stood at the side of the road, arms now folded. "Sure, Leighton. And you're not going into Portland for any other reason."

"I didn't say that—"

"It isn't going to work; you know it isn't."

"I'll find out then, won't I." It was a statement more than a question. "And I really need to get going."

She went back to her car, made another U-turn, and headed back north. He wished she hadn't seen him. What was she doing at the south end this time of morning? It seemed a bit odd. And had she confronted him? This wasn't like Cora.

Thirty minutes later he was on the main road going east. He played *Fiddler,* but it didn't make him laugh as it usually did. A heaviness hung over him, and he was having trouble shaking it.

The closer he got to Portland, the more he thought about Alice. Had he set himself up for disappointment? What if she really wasn't interested, now that she'd had time to think it over, and she didn't know how to tell him? This was probably all a dream, and he'd wake up to find himself back home in bed, with the blankets on the floor.

The traffic thickened as he approached Portland. A layer of haze hovered on the horizon, and a headache started at the base of his neck. He never knew if it was from anxiety or the exhaust fumes. Today he willed the headache to leave. He wasn't going to let anything interfere with his time here.

The new restaurant was in the northwest section of downtown Portland. He found it just fine and presented the idea as he had the other times.

"Yes," the manager said, "I've noticed how some of the restaurants have the display case close to the door and cash register. It *is* a good idea. I'll try it."

After receiving the signature on the dotted line, Leighton hopped back into his truck and put the order on the clipboard. Ah, one more reason to come into town.

Now he had to make the deliveries. He soon discovered he wasn't as young as he used to be and wondered why he hadn't remembered a dolly. Fortunately, they had one at the second restaurant. By the time the last delivery was made, he felt a strong twinge in his lower back. He pulled up to a drive-through espresso shop and ordered a cold latté. It was already three o'clock. He'd head out to Alice's now, but there was one more thing to do.

The night they'd walked, he'd noticed a florist shop up on Fifth. Now he walked out with a bouquet of pink roses. He wasn't sure why he'd picked pink, but she'd worn a pink top that night, and it made her cheeks even rosier. Red would mean more serious intentions, and yellow didn't seem right. Pink was the best choice.

It was going to be four o'clock before he got there, and he knew he'd be caught up in traffic, but he headed out.

Alice answered the door quickly, as if she'd been there waiting. Her eyes widened when she saw the roses.

"How did you know that pink was my favorite color, Leighton?" She hugged him then.

"Just a guess. You look really good."

She wore an apron over beige slacks and a pink-striped

top. She hugged him again before heading to the kitchen to find a vase. "I worried that you were either late getting started, got lost finding the restaurants, or were caught in a traffic jam." Her cheeks were flushed, matching the roses. She kept holding them out to admire.

"None of the above," he said. There was no way he was going to tell her what really happened, with Cora stopping him. "I don't believe it. Here I bought a cellular phone and meant to call you, but plumb forgot I had it."

"You need a cell phone when traveling on the road. I'm glad you have it."

He watched as she poured water in a tall cut-glass vase then added a few grains of sugar. "This is supposed to make them last longer." She put one stem in at a time instead of stuffing them all in at once, as Leighton would have done.

A voice sounded in the hall, and Courtney entered the room. "Oh, Mom, roses!" She bent over and smelled them then turned to Leighton. "How nice to see you again." She held out her hand. "And the roses are beautiful!"

He took her hand. "It's nice seeing you again, too. And when is the baby due?"

"Before Thanksgiving." She smiled. "Figures. It's a boy and boys like to eat. My friend Tina's baby is nine months old, and Isaac eats constantly."

"Guess you know what you're in for," Alice said, not taking her eyes off of Leighton.

"My eldest son and his wife are expecting also. I think he said around New Year's. It's their fourth."

"Fourth?" Courtney seemed as surprised as Alice had when Leighton mentioned he had five children.

"Maybe in time for a tax deduction," Alice said, checking the oven.

"Mom, I'm going to walk over to see Mrs. Rogers. Haven't seen her since I found out I'm carrying a boy."

"Yes, Honey, that's a great idea. You know she'll be delighted to see you."

Leighton watched as the short girl stepped into sandals and went out the door.

"Was her leaving deliberate?" Leighton asked.

"What do you think?"

"I think she didn't want to be around in case I came up and slipped my arm around you and pulled you close and kissed you." He bent down and kissed Alice's forehead, her cheek, then her mouth.

"Hmmm," she said, "I could get real comfortable doing this," and she kissed him back.

"Yes, but we don't know each other yet."

Alice laughed. "You know you're right. I keep forgetting that."

"Things don't happen this fast," Leighton said, meeting her steady gaze. "And I'm not sure I should be left alone with you."

"But the food is cooking—"

"Have you ever heard of shutting a burner off?"

A car horn sounded and Leighton jumped. "Saved by the horn."

They were giggling like two schoolkids when Steven entered the house. "I left early because it's been one hectic day. Honey? Alice? Where is everybody? I know the company's here."

A blushing Alice met him as he rounded the corner. "Courtney's over visiting Mrs. Rogers. Nice to see you, Steven, and glad you came early." She hugged him.

"Oh, hello. You must be Leighton." He held out his hand and Leighton shook it firmly.

"Yeah. The one with the rusted-out truck."

"Oh, it is? I didn't notice."

"Gets rusty at the coast, you know." Leighton was giving him the once-over, just as he knew Steven was doing the same.

"You have no idea how I've looked forward to meeting you. Jeff keeps saying you're an okay sort of guy, and I like to believe the best about people. But Courtney keeps worrying about things, and I didn't know what to think."

"And now?" Alice asked.

"Don't put him on the spot," Leighton said. "Wait until after we play a game of Scrabble. Alice told me it's your favorite pastime on a Sunday afternoon."

"You play?"

"Not really. I mean, it's been a long time."

The evening was pleasant. Leighton had two helpings of Swiss steak and a salad and two pieces of rhubarb pie. He didn't dare tell Alice that he hadn't been eating as well since Cora didn't come to cook. Besides, he wanted her to know he liked her cooking. That was important to most women. Not his sons' wives, though. They both preferred gardening to cooking. But then Alice was old-fashioned.

"Time to play Scrabble," Courtney said, once the dishes were cleared off the table. "I always win, but I might be nice to you." She grinned.

She wasn't nice to him, and Leighton came in last. "That's what happens when you raise boys and end up playing Battleship, War, and Fish."

"Fish!" Steven laughed. "I remember talking Grandma into playing that."

"Let's play," Courtney said. "I'd love to."

It was after ten when Leighton said he'd better get over to John's. "He doesn't even know I'm coming."

"And this is how a cell phone is handy," Alice said. "You could have called him while you were on the road."

He left Alice standing in the doorway. He wanted to kiss her, really kiss her, good night, but opted for a brush of his lips across her cheek. She took his hand again and held on to it as if she didn't want him to leave, either.

"I think we'd better go," Courtney said, walking up behind her mother.

"Everyone's leaving at once," Alice said. "I'm going to be lonely."

Leighton wanted to come back after that remark, but knew he couldn't. "See you soon," he called. "I'll send you a late-night message from John's."

"I'll be waiting."

He opened the truck door when she came running out. "I forgot to thank you for the roses again." She looked into his face. "They're beautiful."

"You're most welcome," he said, a lump coming to his throat. He had to go. It was imperative.

It was a long, lonely ride back across town, and he was glad John was there. He needed to talk to someone. Anyone. The feeling he'd had since he'd first met Alice only intensified tonight, and he knew he was definitely falling in love with her.

ten

Alice spent a restless night. She had wanted to spend more time with Leighton but was glad Courtney and Steven had come, happy that they liked him. In her book, the evening had been a smashing success, especially when they laughed as they played Fish. She knew Courtney would be full of questions and comments tomorrow.

Checking to make sure the burners were all off, Alice caught the scent of roses. She looked at them and marveled at their fragrance, their beauty. She'd have to take Leighton to the Rose Test Gardens in Washington Park. That was definitely on the agenda.

She checked her E-mail, and Leighton had sent a message, as he'd promised. She laughed at the two polar bears hugging.

"Yes, it was a wonderful night," she wrote back. "Courtney didn't say, but I know when she likes someone. You made an impression with her. As for Steven, he's easygoing, so no problem there. Will I see you tomorrow?"

"I'm leaving at five," he wrote back. "Sorry, but when I talked to Luke, he said he thought I'd better get back as soon as possible. There are two men who both want to be boss. It's a long story. I'll explain it sometime."

"I hope it isn't anything too drastic."

"Not anything I can't handle."

"Good night and sleep tight," had been his last message.

Alice slept with those words going through her mind. Sleep tight. No chance of that, not with a hundred thoughts racing through her mind. She knew what Todi meant now. She had not felt this way about Carl. It was entirely different. Did that mean she had not loved him as much? She knew that wasn't true.

She turned on the small lamp beside the bed and read one of her devotionals. It was the one for Wednesday, the day she first met Leighton. "Don't shut the door on new happenings. Rejoice in what God sends your way."

"So, Lord, there is more to life than getting old alone. More than living through the life of your children, anticipating grandbabies. I welcome the challenge."

Leighton sent a greeting card the next morning. Alice printed it out.

At eight he called from Astoria. "Just checking in. I kind of like this phone, but I won't call in traffic."

"I hear the police are cracking down on cell phone users," Alice said.

"Are you going into Spencer Consultants?"

"Yes, Steven said he wanted me there in the afternoon."

"I'll call you tonight, then."

❧

Leighton arrived at the cannery when the first shift was still there. "I understand there've been problems lately, and I want you to know I won't tolerate it. If you don't want to work here, fine. There's the door. I'll give you a week's severance pay. But if you do want the job, then you're going to need to get along with the others. No taking sides. As far as I'm concerned, we're all Americans and we work together. Period. Any questions?"

Nobody raised a hand. "Good. So get to work. And come to me with problems, understand?"

Luke met him outside. "Dad, I think it might work. They listen to you, you know."

"It *has* to work, Son. We've never had this happen before, so let's just not put up with it. Be firm."

He left later to check on the stock in the store and to add the new order to his computer. Alice kept flitting through his mind. He had a plan and would call her tonight.

❧

"I know one thing, Alice," he said when he found her at

home. He had decided to call because he wanted to hear her voice. It soothed him.

"What's that?"

"It's your turn now."

"My turn?"

"Yes. Your turn to come visit me. Bring the kids. I'd love it and so would my sons."

"I'll definitely plan on it, but I'm not sure about Courtney. I think she wants to stay close to home just now. Some expectant mothers don't like to get more than twenty miles from the hospital."

"Good plan."

"And did you resolve the problem at work?"

"I hope so. I had a talk with the troublemakers. I told Luke we just had to pray for peace among our workers. We can't let things fall apart now.

"I've been thinking about you, about wanting to see you again."

"Yes, I've been thinking, too," Alice murmured.

"I need to see you soon. Real soon."

"Before next weekend?" She gripped the receiver, as if it were trying to get away.

"Yes. And I don't want you to worry about driving. I'll send the Bay Shuttle. And Trudy can put you up at one of the most elegant bed and breakfasts you've ever seen."

"Who's Trudy?"

"A shirttail cousin, but I'm not sure whose shirttail."

Alice laughed. "How wonderful it must be to have cousins and lots of aunts and uncles. I never had a big family, and Courtney wished she had a cousin when she was growing up."

"Will you come, then?"

"Yes, I'd like that."

"Fine. When?"

Alice mentally calculated that Steven could do without her. The answering machine could pick up calls, and she didn't need to be at the hospital this week. One call could get someone else to take her shift. She wanted to go immediately. But would that sound too eager?

"I'd like you to come tonight, but I know that isn't possible."

That was all the encouragement Alice needed. "I can be ready tomorrow morning."

"Tomorrow it is." Leighton's voice had a sudden lightness. "I'll check the Bay Shuttle's schedule then get back to you."

Alice clasped her hands as she stared into the growing darkness. He wanted to see her again. He felt the same way she did. And at that thought she jumped to her feet and hurried to the bedroom. What should she take to the beach for a few days' vacation? She had clothes piled on her bed when the phone rang again.

"Mel, the driver, will stop for you tomorrow at noon. I'm meeting you in Seaview, as we'll have a few hours for sightseeing. I'll show you the south end before going to my end of the peninsula and Oysterville."

"Sounds wonderful. I'll be waiting." She gave him her address and directions from the airport, where Mel would be coming from.

Back to the packing. She should take a dressy outfit in case they ate out at an elegant place. Her high-heeled gold sandals and the new pantsuit she'd wear on the shuttle bus. She wanted to look nice when she arrived, as there'd be no chance to change.

When the phone rang, she figured it was Courtney, but it was Leighton again.

"I didn't tell you all that I had on my mind."

"Oh? What is that?"

"That I think you're the neatest lady I've met in a very long while, and I can hardly wait until you get here."

"In the meantime, there's E-mail," Alice murmured.

"Yes, there is. Sleep well tonight. We're going to hike, and I want you to be in good shape."

After the conversation, she tried to get into the novel she'd been reading, but kept reading the same sentence over and over again. Finally, she put the book aside and grabbed her journal.

"Lord, you wouldn't have allowed me to be in this position if You didn't love me and want what is best for my life."

A couple of verses from Hebrews 11 made Alice smile. "Now faith is being sure of what we hope for and certain of what we do not see. This is what the ancients were commended for."

Alice read the verses again and felt tears form.

"Lord, you know I have faith, and because of that faith I am reassured that this is a step You'd have me take."

She closed her Bible and reached for the phone. She better call to let the kids know she would be gone for a few days.

"Mother, are you sure about this?" Courtney said. "Don't you think you should slow down? Let things simmer for a while?"

"Simmer? What do you mean, let things *simmer?* It's already simmering."

"I mean *wait*. Don't rush into anything."

"I'm not rushing. And as for simmering, it's been doing that since the moment I saw him."

"Okay. I just hope it's going to work out."

"If God wants it to, then it will. I'll call you from there. Here, let me give you Leighton's E-mail address so we can keep in touch that way."

"Okay, Mom. Have fun."

"And that's exactly what I intend to do," Alice said as she replaced the receiver. "I'm having an adventure, for sure."

eleven

Alice had changed her mind a dozen times about what to take on the trip. Leighton had warned her that the weather was changeable.

"It can be a nice summer day, seventy degrees or so, then the ocean breezes blow in and it gets foggy and damp."

She had been to the coast many times in her life, but always on the Oregon beaches. She always took older clothes, baggy jeans, sweatshirts, and holey sneakers. But she was meeting Leighton and wanted to look nice.

She packed a pair of blue shorts and a favorite jean shirt with embroidered bears on the pockets. It was the dress she couldn't decide on. Should it be the long flowered crepe or the dressy navy blue linen?

She couldn't believe that he'd insisted on having the Bay Shuttle pick her up.

"But I can drive," Alice had protested again.

"No. It's farther than you realize. You'll hit Chinook, think you're there, then you have the whole peninsula to drive. I'm talking twenty-five miles here."

The shuttle would take her to Seaview, where Leighton would be waiting. "I'll be there before you will, and we'll see the south end, the fishing boats, and the lighthouses, then come on up to my end of the world."

Alice decided on nice butter yellow slacks and a matching jacket, with a lighter shirt. It had been a birthday gift from Agnes.

She wore a gold bracelet, gold rose earrings, and a matching locket. High-heeled sandals completed her outfit. Now all she had to do was wait for the knock at the door. He had assured her that the Bay Shuttle had only the best drivers, and she'd be in good hands.

It was as if her life passed before her eyes while Alice waited. This was turning a new page. She'd thought she was near the end of the book of her life. She'd accomplished many things, and God had blessed her many times over.

She checked to see if her Bible and book of devotionals were in the smaller bag. They were.

Alice heard a car outside. She peeked out the window and saw a young man hop out and head for the house.

"Ms. Adams?" He held out a hand. "I'm your driver. My name's Mel."

She nodded. "I'm ready, Mel." She suddenly felt uneasy, without knowing why. "Let me check the burners one last time."

He chuckled as he took the two bags and headed for the small van.

"I remember reading a joke in *Reader's Digest* once," Mel said once they were on the road heading west. "This woman always thought she'd left the iron on, and she and her husband'd have to turn around and go back to check. Then one year, as they were driving down the freeway, she said she knew she'd left the iron on. Her husband stopped the car and went to the back where everything was packed. 'Nope! You didn't. Here it is.' And he held the iron up for her to see."

Alice laughed. "That's a good one."

"And a smart husband," Mel added.

Alice leaned back against the cushion and envisioned Leighton coming to meet her. What would they say to each other? Would they be awkward? She felt like a girl, not the mature woman she'd always projected.

"Have you been to the peninsula before?" Mel asked, breaking into her reverie.

"Never."

She wanted to say she'd like anything if Leighton were there, but instead said, "Do you know Leighton Walker, the man I'm meeting?"

Mel met her gaze in the rearview mirror. "Alice, everyone

knows everyone there, especially people like the Walkers, who've been in the oyster business since the beginning of time. Leighton's a community leader, too, and that means a lot to a small place like the peninsula."

"Oh. I suppose I should have guessed that."

"I worked for him one time at the cannery."

"And how was that?"

"Good job, but I don't like smelling like oysters all day. You'll see people walking around in tall rubber boots in town, and you'll smell 'em a mile away."

Alice laughed. "I can hardly wait." She leaned back then remembered the bag by the front door.

"I forgot my hat!" she blurted. "And my tennis shoes. Oh, no."

"Too late to worry about that now. Besides, there are places to buy things like that. People always forget something. Usually it's a jacket in the summer. They expect it to be hot all day, and it just isn't."

Alice was the only one on the Bay Shuttle, a rare occurrence, according to Mel. "We've gotten so busy with the shuttle that they've added another van."

They chitchatted for a while, then Alice read a book. She also enjoyed the scenery along the way.

"We're getting close to the Astoria Bridge. Surely you've been across it."

"No, I can't say that I have." Alice's breath caught as Mel drove around a curve. Suddenly there they were, high up over the Columbia River, with water in every direction as far as she could see. She shivered. "This reminds me of the suspension bridge at Canon City, Colorado. It scared me half to death when we walked across it. At least I have the safety of a car."

"Yeah, that right? This is one of the longest single-lane truss bridges ever built. Now we're almost level with the water. Isn't that a spectacular view?"

"It's gorgeous," Alice said, her stomach settling down. "It reminds me of a ride they had at the old Jantzen Beach

Amusement Park I went to as a kid."

They were soon across the river and on solid road, passing through a tunnel, the town of Chinook, and finally, Seaview.

"I see Leighton's Chevy," Mel said as he was waiting to turn left. Alice felt her heart thud madly. There was Leighton, standing next to his truck, long and lean in Levis and a plaid shirt, a cap on his head, as if that would hold back his unruly hair.

She didn't remember getting out of the van or realize that her luggage had been put in the back of Leighton's truck. All she could do was watch him, his manner, and the way he smiled, and she knew. Knew that her life would forever be entwined with his.

He pulled her close briefly, then, hand in hand, they went to the truck. "I didn't think you'd ever arrive."

Alice felt her cheeks flush. "Mel made good time."

"You know what I meant. I'm sure he did. I came thirty minutes early just in case he made even better time. I regret I don't have the car, but it needed a brake job. I'll pick it up tomorrow."

"It was a lovely drive, and I sure don't mind riding in a truck."

"And it's a lovely day. We're not always so blessed with sunshine." He helped her into the truck, his hand lingering on her arm. "Luke had a fit when I said I was picking you up in the old Chev."

"I like the truck. I can see even better."

"You always look at things from the positive angle, don't you?" Leighton leaned over and impulsively kissed her cheek. "I like that."

"I never thought about it."

"It's true."

He thought of Nancy, who complained daily, and of Cora, who got cranky at times.

"Let's go for our sight-seeing drive. We'll get out and walk to North Head, then go over to the restaurant I was telling you about."

"Whatever you have planned is fine," Alice said. "I'll enjoy every moment."

"What did your daughter say about your coming?"

Alice laughed. "Courtney didn't say a whole lot. She worries about me, though."

"As a good daughter should."

"And your boys?"

Leighton shrugged. "They knew you were coming, and that's about it. I don't tell them all my business, just as they don't tell me all of theirs."

"Sounds typical of the male gender."

"Don't go getting all stereotypical on me."

Alice stole a look out of the corner of her eye. "It's true and you know it."

"You'll meet Luke at the cannery tonight. We'll drop by before closing."

Alice thought of Courtney's words. She didn't want Leighton to know what she'd said about getting hurt. That was like fishing for a commitment, and she was far from wanting to do that.

Golden sunshine, a true gift for the day, filled the truck. When Leighton rolled his window down, Alice sniffed the ocean air. There was nothing like it anywhere.

"I hope you can stay several days," he said.

"I'm not sure. Do I have to know now?"

"Of course not."

"I can stay two days, anyway, if you want me that long."

Leighton turned and met her gaze. He'd just pulled into the parking lot and shut the engine off. "If I want you—"

"Company should never stay more than three days, my mother always said. I don't want you to tire of me."

"I won't, and I sure know that Trudy won't."

They walked down the winding path that led to the lighthouse. Through the thick growth of trees, Alice caught glimpses of a sandy beach, waves splashing up, and dots that were people.

"Benson Beach. Where the campers go," Leighton explained. They stopped, and he held her hand gently. "We can go there sometime, too. There's so much to do."

The lighthouse was around the next bend, and Alice drew in a sharp breath. With a red top, it stood like the commanding beacon it was.

"We can tour it."

But Alice didn't tell him about her fear of heights or that she hadn't once flown in an airplane. "I'd like to stand down here and just watch the ocean, if that's okay."

"Remember, I've been here many times. It's your call."

They leaned against a chain-link fence and looked south then north. The water was a china blue, the waves white and fierce. A wind picked up, and Alice breathed in. Leighton's hand still held hers, tighter now.

"It is beautiful. Like Paradise must be."

After the drive back into town, Leighton pulled up next to a large building. A sign beamed from the third floor.

"Here's where you'll get the best clam chowder ever."

As they looked out on the water and watched children running from the waves, Alice savored the chowder, stirred her iced tea with a straw, and wondered if this was just a dream. She could hardly wait for Courtney and Steven to come here also.

"Look, a car's getting towed," Leighton said. "People forget how difficult it is to navigate in soft sand. They're always getting stuck."

"Do you drive on the beach?"

"Sure. Always have. We could go, but the tide's in and it's best to wait until later, when it's out."

The waitress came, offering them dessert menus.

"The Columbia Sludge Pie is awfully good," Leighton said, but Alice knew she couldn't eat another bite. She'd been like this, eating so little ever since that afternoon they'd met.

"We can come back later for dessert," she said.

"Sounds fine to me."

Moments later they were outside, walking the boardwalk that ran above the sand, still affording walkers a view of the water and all the activity.

"I can see why you love it here," Alice finally said. "Such a far cry from the city."

They drove what Leighton called the back road until they reached Oysterville.

"The whole town is on the historical social register?" she asked. That sounded pretty important.

Leighton nodded. "Sure is. It was a booming town in its day. Back in the late 1800s and up until 1920 or so. Had its heyday, so to speak, but that was almost a century ago. Now we have the old church that has vespers during the summer and weddings with receptions in the old schoolhouse. And every year before Christmas, there's an old-fashioned party with more food than you could possibly try, a Santa, gift exchanges, and drawings for various products from local merchants."

"It's breathtakingly wonderful! After living in the city, I had no idea such a place could even exist."

Leighton pulled up in front of a Victorian house painted a creamy beige with a forest green trim. "This is it! My abode."

Alice stared in fascination. Huge trees bordered the front yard. The grass was thick, green, and lush. A picket fence outlined the property.

"This is where you've always lived?"

"Since I was two."

"It's wonderful."

The bay was at full tide, and Alice drew in deep breaths. "I love it!" She looked over at Leighton and saw an almost bemused look on his craggy face. "What? Are you laughing at me?"

"Leighton!" A voice called from the open doorway of the house. "I have dinner ready." A short woman with dark hair pulled back into a tight bun looked at Leighton, then noticed Alice.

"I didn't know you were bringing a guest."

Alice felt her face go hot. Who was this person standing on the porch, acting as if she owned the place? As if she belonged to Leighton or perhaps he belonged to her?

"I'm Alice Adams." She stepped forward and offered her hand. "I've never been to Oysterville, and it's a wonderful, delightful place!"

The woman frowned then took Alice's hand. "I'm Cora Benchley. I've been housekeeper, cook, nanny—you name it—for the past fifteen years since Aunt Rita died."

Alice felt the smile freeze on her face. This was the woman Leighton had mentioned that first night at the restaurant, and she definitely looked as if she owned the place.

twelve

Alice felt uncomfortable as the woman scrutinized her. Had Leighton known she would be here? She obviously felt she belonged, and it was as if Alice were trespassing on her property.

Leighton, also feeling uncomfortable, finally found his voice. "Cora, why are you here? I hadn't planned on eating at home tonight."

"I like to cook. You know that." She swept her hand toward the immense porch. "It's simple fare. A pot of clam chowder, thick with clams and chunks of potatoes, bacon, and lots of butter and cream, just the way you like it. There's also hot corn bread. And I made a blackberry crisp from berries I picked last summer and put in the freezer. Besides, Leight, you left everything in an absolute shambles."

Alice swallowed hard. This woman clearly knew what Leighton liked to eat, and it appeared she pretty well ran the place. She also probably knew that Alice was coming but had decided to ignore the fact.

"Are you staying here, my dear?" Cora asked then with the slightest hint of sarcasm in her lilting voice.

"Oh, I don't think so," Alice said, once she found her voice.

"Leighton?" She turned to face him.

"No, Cora. She'll be over at Trudy's bed and breakfast. I thought that was much more appropriate. I just brought her here to see the place and Oysterville. We're going by the cannery before it gets dark, to see if Luke is there."

"So you won't be eating?" Her face showed her keen disappointment.

"Actually, we had dinner at the Lightship."

"Ah, well, the chowder is better the second day, anyway. As for the corn bread, I'll just take it home with me."

Alice wanted to disappear. This had not happened very many times in her life, but this was one of them. Why hadn't Leighton told her about the woman who kept his house? She surely had designs on him—no doubt about it—and as was so often with men, Leighton now seemed flustered about the whole thing.

"Am I going to meet your boys?" Alice heard herself saying, not liking the uncomfortable silence.

"Boys?" Cora looked perplexed.

"Not tonight," Leighton said.

"Oh, I assumed they were coming, since Cora cooked and cleaned."

Cora whirled around. "I don't tend to the boys now, but Leighton still needs looking out for and caring. A whole lot of caring."

Alice took a deep breath. "I'm sure he does," she said, suddenly wishing she wore Levis, as Cora did, feeling out of place in the dressy yellow slack set.

"Listen, I think we'd better get on over by the cannery, then I'll take you to Trudy's."

Cora hurried to the kitchen, and seconds later the sound of the refrigerator door opening and closing told them that the dinner, so carefully prepared, was now being put away.

"It was nice meeting you," Alice called out, as Leighton held the door open, his hand brushing against her shoulder. She jumped aside.

"Same here," the voice called from the kitchen.

"She knew you were coming," Leighton said in a low voice. "She also knows I told her I didn't need her working for me anymore. She's acting like she's taken leave of her senses."

Alice knew why Cora had acted like that, but she didn't dare say so. She walked down the steps, careful not to trip in the high heels. *How inappropriate,* she thought for the second time that day, *to bring such footwear to the beach.*

"Forget the way Cora acted. Don't let her ruin your visit."

"I'm not sure what to think."

Leighton scowled. "She's an old friend. Nothing more. She just likes to run things. Always been that way."

Again, Alice didn't comment. Men could be so blind.

"You'll love the bed and breakfast," Leighton said, slipping his arm casually around her shoulder. Alice wanted to lean into him, wanted to feel the safe comfort of his arms, but she couldn't. Especially now that she knew about Cora. There was more to Leighton than she first thought.

"Cora means well," he said, as if reading her mind. "She gets a bit bossy. I've put up with it over the years, and that's why I said something to her the other day."

"She loves you," Alice said. "It's very clear."

"Loves me!" He looked perplexed again. "Now, why on earth would you think that?"

"Oh, Leighton. If she's been keeping your house and taking care of you for a long while, she's not about to give it all up now."

"She's a friend. She knows that. I've always paid her for her work and the cooking. It isn't as if it's gratis."

"Cora wants more than money."

"That's nonsense!" He closed her truck door, and soon they were driving north again. The cannery was closed down for the night, which he thought strange. "I'll look into it tomorrow. Besides, it's late and you need to get to your place for the night. 'Tomorrow is another day,' as my mother used to say."

Alice nodded. She was tired. They'd done a lot, and she'd been busy since six in the morning. It was time to relax and kick off these ridiculous sandals. Tomorrow she'd buy a pair of sensible tennis shoes. She'd noticed a store back in Long Beach that must sell them.

"I've had a wonderful time," she said as the truck now headed south. "I'm looking forward to doing more sight-seeing tomorrow."

"And so we shall." He slipped his arm around the back of the seat.

"Tomorrow is going to be a wonderful, beautiful day," Alice murmured. "I can hardly wait."

They drove up a long, winding driveway that was wooded and secluded, then pulled up in front of a huge house with three stories. "This is it!" Leighton said.

"It's a mansion!"

"With a view. And the best cook you could ever hope to meet."

"I won't tell Cora you said that."

Leighton's face grew serious. "That's enough about Cora."

He led Alice to the sitting room that overlooked the bay. The tide was in, and it looked peaceful and serene—a sea of glass with the hills in the background. A formal parlor was to her right. An older man sat in a burgundy wing chair, reading a magazine. He nodded. "Nice night, isn't it?"

"Yes, it is," Leighton said.

Trudy appeared, drying her hands on a blue-and-white-striped apron. "Leighton, you've brought your guest. I'm so glad this was a slow weekend. No festivals, fairs, or parades." She laughed, and Leighton chuckled.

"Apparently a lot goes on around here in the summer," Alice said.

"Oh, yes," Trudy said. "From Memorial Day until the end of September, I'm usually filled to capacity. But I love it!"

Leighton set Alice's suitcase down.

"How about I give you the complete tour in the morning?" Trudy said. "Perhaps you'll want to sit out in one of the Adirondack chairs and watch the sunrise."

"I'll be back over for breakfast," Leighton said. "I'll let Trudy show you to your room." He leaned over and kissed Alice's cheek.

"Yes, do come early," Trudy said. "You know how you like my cranberry-orange muffins." She hugged him impulsively.

"Is eight soon enough?"

"Better make it seven thirty."

The two watched as Leighton strode toward the door and left without looking back.

"Come, Dear, let's go to your room on the second floor. I'll carry your luggage. I'm quite used to it, you know."

Alice followed Trudy up the winding staircase, with its highly polished oak banister and wide, deep steps. Trudy paused in front of a door with a whimsical sign that read *Garden Room*.

"Here it is. It's perfect for one guest. You still get a queen-sized feather bed, though."

Alice looked at the large four-poster bed with a slatted head-board and a blue-and-green gingham cover. A nightstand with a pitcher decorated a table in one corner. The drapes were pulled back with a sash that matched the comforter.

"It's so lovely; I hate to muss the bed," Alice said, noticing the private bathroom to the left. "I'm going to just love it here."

"Nothing's too good for Leighton. Heaven knows that man's been through a knothole twice."

"Everyone must know Leighton," Alice said.

"Oh, my, yes. It's a small town, you know." Trudy patted Alice's arm. "It would take some getting used to for a city gal."

"You seem to know Leighton so well. Are you related?" Alice said, remembering that Leighton had referred to Trudy as a shirttail cousin.

"Cousins twice removed, I think, but I've never figured it out. I've known him since the day he was born. His parents were of fine stock. They don't come any better than the Walkers."

Alice knew she shouldn't ask, but she had to know. "I sup-pose you know Cora, then?"

"Cora Benchley? Oh, yes." Trudy leaned over and fluffed up both pillows. "She's had her eye on Leighton since she returned from Cathlamet. I expect that's been at least fifteen years ago now."

"I know she's in love with Leighton."

Trudy nodded then met Alice's steady gaze. "Yes, I'm afraid that's the truth of it. Though Leighton is absolutely blind to it. That's a man for you!"

Alice wasn't sure how to respond to Trudy's statement. "I'm going to sleep well in this room," she said.

"Glad you like it. Leighton chose it because it looks out over the bay. In the morning, you'll have the most beautiful sunrise you've ever seen."

She leaned over and turned down the gingham quilt. "If you need anything, just let me know, okay?"

She closed the door behind herself, and Alice was alone for the first time since early morning. She needed time and space to function. A time for prayer and meditation at the end of the day helped her gather her thoughts. It also helped her face any problems that had come along.

Cora. Was she a problem? Perhaps not. Cora loved Leighton, and he probably loved her but couldn't see the forest for the trees. Alice was just a friend, and though she got tingly at his touch, she knew nothing would come of their friendship. How could it, with the distance between them? Surely he had realized that by now. And yet. . .

She opened her suitcase and chose a long floral dress with cap sleeves. It would do for lounging, and she'd probably wear this to breakfast in the morning. Leighton. He had more than one woman who loved him. What on earth did he see in Alice? She knew nothing about the oyster business. She didn't know his children nor his late wife. She hadn't even brought proper clothing to the beach. And here she had to pretend to know about this life.

Alice sat on the edge of the bed, loving the soft fullness of the quilt. A small bathroom was off the bedroom, and the bathtub looked inviting—especially when she saw the bath oils and huge, fluffy towels.

After a long, leisurely soak in the huge claw-foot bathtub, Alice sat on the edge of the bed and thought about all that had happened in the past four days. It seemed impossible. How could she, Alice Adams, be in this situation? She had led such a simple life in the years since Carl's death. Now she was embarked on something that almost frightened her. Could she cope? Did she even want to?

She dried her hair with the big, thick towel, then brushed several strokes. Her journal and Bible were the only things left in the suitcase. She wrote in her journal when things troubled her, and this was beginning to trouble her. She had no right to come, to step in and take over for a woman who loved Leighton, who had obviously loved him since his wife died. Maybe even before. How could she fight that? Did she really want to?

She opened the Bible randomly and a highlighted verse jumped out at her: "Teach me your way, O Lord; lead me in a straight path."

"But, Lord, do I want to follow? How do I know? How can I know this is the right step? And what about Courtney and my grandbaby-to-be? How can I think of leaving them, should it come to that?"

She slid under the soft comforter. Tomorrow was going to be another day like today had been. Something told her she'd better get a full night's sleep so she'd be fresh and ready. But would she ever really be ready to step in and be Leighton's helpmate? Is this what God expected of her?

She closed her eyes and prayed: "Not my will, but Thy will, Lord. Help me to know what You'd have me do, what You want me to be. Amen."

thirteen

Cora was waiting when Leighton got home. Somehow he knew she would be. The house was dark except for a faint ray of moonlight.

"Leight—" Her voice broke.

He turned the lamp on beside the recliner.

"No. Shut it off, please. I can sit in the dark and think, just as I can sit in the dark and converse."

"Okay." He sat in the chair, almost afraid to go any closer.

"I've known you a long time."

"Yes," he said finally.

"It's a long time to put into a relationship that is clearly going nowhere."

"Now, Cora. That's just it. There has never been a relationship, not to my way of thinking."

"You took me out to dinner that one time."

"It was your birthday, if I remember right."

"Yes, well, Mama warned me that things were one-sided." She laughed. "And you know what? My mother was right. But I'm stubborn. You saw me training that horse that wouldn't let a soul near it."

"Yes, you were fantastic with that Morgan. Cute little filly, wasn't she?"

"Yes, she was. I fit in here. I know everyone. The peninsula is my life. Yours, too. I also know that you like just a touch of starch in your shirts, you eat dinner at six most nights, and you prefer the turkey stuffed with bread dressing instead of corn bread." She laughed then. "Remember when I put oysters in and nobody would eat it?"

He remembered only too well. Cora, who hadn't been with them long, burst into tears and refused to eat dinner.

"We have memories, and that's what you build a relationship on." Her voice grew louder. "Not some person you meet one time and get all excited about."

Leighton nodded. "You're right. There is something to say for continuity."

She got up from the love seat, moving a dining room chair over next to the recliner. He knew she wanted him to reach out, to touch her, to say he'd been wrong, that he'd reconsider. But he couldn't do what she wanted.

"Cora, you're right about a lot of this. And maybe I need advice, but you're not the one to ask."

"It hasn't stopped you in the past." Her voice came out stilted, not sounding like her at all. "We can still be friends, can't we?"

"I suppose we can. You know I love the peninsula. The bay. My house. The oysters. My life here in general. How can I give this up and move elsewhere?"

"Heavens!" she blurted out. "Why would you even consider such a thing?"

"I'm not sure. It's just that sometimes I feel lonely, and life is short when you get right down to it. God never gave us any guarantees about how long our time is here on earth."

"That He didn't."

"I've thought about my child, my little sick darling who died in my arms. I think about my boys and being there for them, and hoping against hope that Aaron might come driving into the yard someday."

"And he just might."

"But there's a missing link, and I may have found what I didn't know I was even looking for."

Cora jumped to her feet. "Why can't *I* be the missing link?"

When he said nothing, she kept the ball rolling. "It's okay to be friends first. All the books and articles say that."

Leighton sighed. How had he gotten into this conversation, anyway? She didn't understand. She would never understand. Love couldn't be forced, and what he felt for her was only gratitude. Appreciation. Admiration.

"Maybe Alice isn't the right one. I don't think she wants to upset the apple cart any more than I do. We both have our lives in different places. Yes, we enjoy each other's company and, yes, we do seem to have a lot in common, but maybe it isn't enough. Who knows? I certainly don't have the answers."

"What exactly are you saying, Leight?"

He leaned forward, putting his head into his hands. "I think I've just come to realize that I need, or maybe I should say *want,* a helpmate. Alice helped me see that. Here I've been so caught up with raising my kids and the job taking every spare minute. Now it's as if I never had time to enjoy life."

"And so you and she are enjoying life?"

"No, that's just it. I'm not sure about her and me. It's just an awareness that made me understand my needs."

"So what I said is right. We can build a relationship. It *is* possible. I've always been here; you know that."

"Yes, I know. And I appreciate all you've done—"

"Appreciate?" She paced across the room.

"Yes, appreciate." He could feel her breath as her face got closer. "I think I'm going to date for a while."

"Oh. That's what this is about. You want my advice about dating? Is that why you're telling me this?"

"Well, yes. As a friend."

"Leighton Walker, I think you are probably the most stupid man I've ever seen. Have you listened to anything I've said? Have I ever meant anything to you at all?"

"Cora? Why are you yelling?"

"Because I'm tired. It's been a trying day, and I'm going home!"

She spun around and banged out the door before he could even rise.

The gravel spit as her car turned and headed out the winding driveway.

Leighton sat in the darkness. Cora didn't understand how it was. He did not love her. How could he pretend something he did not feel? Pretense never had worked for him. He knew women did it all the time, but not men. Maybe he should talk to Trudy. She might listen to him without getting angry.

He did not move. There was nothing he wanted more than to sit here and to think about his life. It was dark out now, and an occasional light from a car on the highway across the bay and on the road to Bay Center sparked like a firefly. Not that he'd seen fireflies, but he'd heard about them. And someday he might see a real one.

Finally he rose and paced across the room. His mind was in a turmoil. He knew he did not love Cora. He also knew how he felt around Alice. She made him feel like singing, and it had been a very long time since he'd had that feeling. Was that wrong? Or had God been waiting to show him there could be joy in life, and why didn't Leighton just reach out for it?

ঌ

Cora sped down the driveway and back toward town. Her house was north of Leighton's on Stackpole Road, but she wasn't going home. She could not go home. She had to talk to someone, and as she often did when problems hit, she'd find her cousin, Meredith, and ask her advice. Of course, Meredith would agree with Cora's mother that she had given enough time and energy to this relationship. Tonight's conversation only backed that up. But how could she give up the only man she'd ever loved?

The darkened house made Cora consider just leaving without their talk, but she couldn't. She knew there would be no sleep for her tonight.

She grabbed the key from under the pot of petunias and let herself in. "Meredith? It's just me. Put away your gun."

"Cora?" a sleepy voice called from the bedroom, then a woman appeared in the doorway. "What are you doing here this late?"

"It's only ten."

"But I have to get up and go to Astoria at seven tomorrow."

"I know and I'm sorry, but you're the only one I can talk to."

"Not Leighton."

"Well, yes, as a matter of fact—"

"Listen, Cora, you've never listened to any advice I've given you, so why should I think you'll listen now?" The tall, buxom woman turned on a small light and put the teakettle on.

"Because I just might listen this time."

"Yeah, sure." She pulled a chair out and eased into it. "I think you should move away from here. Go as far away as you can so you won't be tempted to come back every weekend."

"Away? Where, pray tell?"

"How about Bar Harbor, Maine?"

"Maine!"

"You like the water, so you'd have water there."

"But that's over three thousand miles away!"

"And that's what you need—distance."

Cora got up and took the singing kettle off the burner. "No. Maybe I'll go visit Aunt Joan in Virginia."

"I don't mean visit."

"I can't start my life over. I'm forty-two!"

"I know how old you are. I'm just a year behind."

"You're not married yet."

"And I'm not pining for a man who will never, ever love me, either."

They had instant coffee, jelly rolls, peanuts, and everything else Meredith could drag out of the refrigerator.

"I haven't had a night feast like this forever," Meredith said.

"Not since the last time I got you out of bed."

The two were still talking at midnight. Meredith, who was even more organized and opinionated than Cora, had it mapped out. Cora would call the travel bureau and get the first plane heading out of Oysterville. She would look for work in Virginia, and she would not have contact with anyone here.

"If separation doesn't make him realize how much he misses you, nothing will."

Cora would not tell Leighton she was leaving. She'd leave her house empty, take a suitcase of clothes, and Meredith would feed her cat. What happened when Leighton found his refrigerator without food would be his problem, not hers.

"I think this is a wise move," Meredith said. "Though I'll miss you something fierce."

"You can come visit."

"Yeah, I suppose I could do that." Meredith, who taught school, was out for the summer and usually planned at least one trip over her vacation.

Cora hugged her good-bye and headed for home. Now she could sleep. Or could she?

The best-laid plans ran through her mind as the clock turned to one, two, then three. Finally, she got up and put some music on. The Dixie Chicks sang "Once You've Loved Somebody."

She wasn't sure what she would do, but neither Virginia nor Bar Harbor, Maine was the answer. She could never leave and admit defeat. Never.

fourteen

A morning sunrise awakened Alice, its brilliance summoning her. For a moment she forgot where she was. With sudden delight, she jumped from bed and looked out the window at the sky in explosive reds and oranges. She'd never seen anything like it. Of course, the fact that she never was up at this hour might have something to do with it. It wasn't even six o'clock yet.

She padded to the bathroom and looked in the mirror. Her eyes were puffy from sleep. Obviously she had slept well, not waking once, though she had been sure she would. It had been so quiet. No sounds of cars zipping by, no sirens in the middle of the night, no lights or phone calls. Silence. Golden silence.

Alice opened her journal and wrote a few lines at the top. "I'm ready and waiting for whatever is to be."

Her Bible devotional was surprisingly just what she needed to hear. "Consider it pure joy, my brothers, whenever you face trials of many kinds."

"I don't know if I'm being faced with trials, but I am ready for whatever this day brings, for whatever You want me to do."

The scent of coffee came up the stairs and entered through the register. Warm air also came through the intricate metal register on the floor. Alice had not felt chilled, but the warm air was nice.

Alice opened the door to the deck just off her bedroom and slipped outside. It was cold. Brisk. She grabbed the small throw blanket at the foot of the bed and wrapped it around herself as she watched the changing sky from the Adirondack chair.

She had two choices for the day. The beige silk slack set,

totally not right for here, or the long jumper that would be better and more suitable. She decided on the jumper, a pink blouse with a touch of lace, and the sandals that would be replaced with tennis shoes.

Now Alice smelled something baking. Probably the cranberry muffins. There was a tap on her door as a cheery voice called out. "I have coffee if you'd like. I don't expect Leighton until seven or so."

Alice hopped up from the chair and opened the door. Trudy came in with a tray laden with not only coffee but a plate of fresh fruit. Mango slices, grapes, apple wedges, and blueberries.

"Just to tide you over."

"But how did you know I was up?"

"I heard the floors creak. I shouldn't have told you my little secret." Trudy beamed as she poured a cup of coffee. A tiny pitcher contained cream, and a small ceramic pig was filled with sugar. "I bought this from a lady who comes from North Dakota each summer and sells her pottery at our local Fourth of July festival. Isn't he charming?"

Alice nodded and poured sugar into a spoon. "I must get one of these." She knew Courtney would love it, since she had just started collecting pigs.

Trudy beamed. "I just so happen to have a few extra. I like to keep small gifts on hand to give my guests as a remembrance of their stay at Trudy's Bed and Breakfast on the Bay."

"The coffee is wonderful and the fruit a real treat."

"I'll leave you to your own devices. Come down when you're ready." Trudy looked elegant in her white apron that fit over a green-and-white-striped pinafore dress. Everything about this trip was elegant.

Alice sat, sipping her coffee and looked out at the bay. So beautiful and quaint and quiet. How could she not want to stay here? But, of course, she was thinking about things that probably wouldn't be, anyway. Leighton had a relationship with that Cora woman, who obviously adored him and his family. How could Alice look for a future with him? Besides, it was too early to think about such things. She had come to spend time with him and sightsee, and that's what she was going to do.

She left half of the fruit, put on the sandals, and took the tray back downstairs. A girl of ten or so was in the kitchen cutting wedges of toast.

"Good morning," she called out when Alice brought the tray into the kitchen. "I'm helping Aunt Trudy."

"How many other guests are there? It's so quiet; I thought I was the only one."

"We have three other rooms filled. Newlyweds, someone celebrating their anniversary, and a lady by herself, like you."

Alice walked out onto a deck that ran across the entire back of the house. A goose called to his mate in the distance. Such a peaceful setting. Courtney and Steven would have to come here to see the beauty of this place. Perhaps it could be an anniversary gift.

She sat in one of the lawn chairs, drawing her feet up under herself. She felt as if she could stay in this same spot all day. How fortunate to have met Leighton, and how amazing that he brought her here to share this with her. How could she ever go home again?

"There you are!" Leighton stood over her, leaned down, and kissed her cheek, just as he had last night. "I'm early, but Trudy called to say you were up and so here I am."

"Oh, Leighton." She felt all breathless. "This view is heavenly. Thanks so much for bringing me here."

"I thought you would like it."

"Trudy brought coffee and fruit to my room, and I slept through the whole night. I can't even remember the last time I did that."

She knew she was rambling, but she felt comfortable with this kind man and the way he was looking at her, all smiles. Did he feel the same toward her?

"We'll eat one of Trudy's breakfasts fit for a queen, and

you may not want to eat the rest of the day."

Alice chuckled. "I'm already thinking that. How can I eat more?"

They sat watching the bay and the sun behind the hills. The silence was comfortable, as if they knew no words needed to be spoken.

Leighton spoke first. "Your face shows your pleasure, and that brings me such satisfaction. You have no idea how much."

"Where are we going today? One thing I need to do is buy a pair of tennis shoes. I thought at that store back in Long Beach."

Leighton nodded. "Yes, I suppose those shoes wouldn't be good for hiking to Cape D. It's an uphill climb, and tennis shoes would definitely give you better traction."

"I left the bag with my old tennis shoes at home."

"We don't have to hike, of course."

"Oh, but I want to. I haven't hiked much since, well, since Carl died, but I do the aerobics at the pool, so I'm in shape."

His eyes twinkled. "And in good shape, I might add."

"Breakfast time!" A small silver bell rang from the dining area.

"Doesn't that smell good!"

Platters were filled with sausage, bacon, and slices of ham, along with a stack of pancakes and another of Belgian waffles. Plates of honey, jams, real butter, hash browns, and a spinach frittata covered the lace-covered tablecloth. The dishes were an elegant porcelain with a tiny red rose pattern.

"Who would have expected this at the beach?" Alice exclaimed. "Perhaps my gold sandals aren't so out of place."

A young couple entered the dining room, holding hands. They nodded. "Hi. We're here on our tenth anniversary."

"And this is my first time here," Alice said, looking toward Leighton.

For the next several minutes, a conversation was carried on, and Alice heard how life was in Flagstaff, Arizona.

"There are two things you must do while here," Leighton told the couple. He stirred sugar into his coffee. "Go to the north end to Leadbetter Point. It's like Cape Cod, I've been told, because it's flat, but it has more dune grass. If you have binoculars, take them along. There are more birds in that area than anywhere else on the peninsula. In order to get there, you'll go through the old town of Oysterville. That's also worth a stop."

"Which is where Leighton lives and owns an oyster cannery," Trudy added.

"The south end has more hills, good hikes, and a great panorama of the ocean. You can also see clear to the north end of the peninsula on a nice day. Pick up one of the visitors' guides from the newspaper office in Long Beach."

"I have plenty of guides right here," Trudy said. She fetched one from an end table in the parlor. "This can tell you lots of things to do and places to go."

The couple beamed. "Thanks so much."

Alice tasted the frittata and chose a slice of bacon and a muffin.

They all started eating and it was quiet, but only for a few minutes.

"We'll be back," the young man said, pushing away from the table. "I won this vacation from my company, so time is limited. We can take in one of your suggestions, then we have to leave for Seattle to catch an early flight home."

"But this has been elegant," his wife said, a tiny woman no more than five feet tall.

"I can't eat another bite," Alice said, folding the napkin and setting it on her plate.

"There's always tomorrow," Leighton added. "I bet there will be something new to try then."

Alice went back upstairs for a wrap and her purse.

"We'll go to the store first so you can find some walking shoes," Leighton said.

Trudy hollered for them to wait a minute. Seconds later, she came back with a shoe box, and inside was a pair of blue deck shoes. "I thought you might be able to wear these. Someone left them here, and when I mailed her a note, she said not to bother with sending them back. They're brand-new."

They fit and Alice thanked her.

Trudy handed Leighton a small white paper sack. "Just something else to take along."

"What's in that sack?" Alice asked, noticing that Leighton stowed it in the backseat.

"A box lunch."

"Packed by Trudy?"

"None other."

"She does everything so effortlessly."

He looked over and grinned. "That's just the way it appears. We're all laid back here on the peninsula, or hadn't you noticed?"

Except Cora, Alice wanted to say. Cora had managed to get a barb in, letting Alice know she would have a fight on her hands should she pursue this relationship. But Alice was enjoying herself. She wasn't going to let herself get serious about Leighton. His place was here, just as hers was in Portland. There was no harm in an occasional visit, and when he came to town, they could take in a movie, or she might fix a dinner of her famous baked chicken.

"You're smiling. What's on your mind?"

Alice leaned forward. "Oh, just thinking about life in general, realizing we never know what lies around the next bend."

Leighton reached over and covered her hand with his. "I think God likes to surprise us, don't you?"

"Yes, indeed I do."

"Tomorrow we'll have to go to the vespers at the Oysterville Church. You'll love the service."

"Is that the church you attend regularly?"

He frowned for a moment. "No. There's only an afternoon service during the summer months. Other times I attend a community church, when my schedule allows."

Alice thought about her church and how much she would miss her friends, her daughter, the new baby, if she ever left. And there would be more children, because Courtney said she wanted a large family.

"There you go again. It's as if I'm not here. You keep thinking about other things."

"And that's rude of me. I'm sorry."

The ride down what Leighton called the back road was scenic, with large trees and woodsy areas. A house could be seen now and then, and if she looked close, she caught a glimpse of blue water from the bay, but it was mostly brush and foliage.

"I cannot imagine how I lived my whole life in Portland and never knew about this spot. I like it. It isn't commercialized, as so many of the beach towns are in Oregon."

"We like it that way."

"Are we going to Cape Disappointment now?"

"No, not yet. We'll go to Waikiki Beach while the sun's out. The weather is fickle here; it could be foggy and cold by noon."

"At least we don't need to stop at that little shopping center." Alice wiggled her toes inside the new blue deck shoes, which would be perfect for hiking.

Alice sat back again and felt her body relax. She wouldn't go off and think about things he knew nothing about. She would share just a bit of her life with him.

"The first time I hiked was in Florence, Oregon. I went with Todi. We went every year the minute the trails were dry."

"Todi?"

"An old school friend. We were inseparable. Then I married Carl, and the air force took us all over."

"Tell me about Carl, if you can."

Alice felt sudden warmth. Of course she could. She liked talking about Carl and the wonderful years they'd shared, the day they brought Courtney home.

"I was married young. And you?"

"That's not fair." Leighton scowled. "This is supposed to be about you."

"I just wanted to compare."

"Okay. I guess that's fair. I married young also. Nancy and I went all through school together, but we never dated until our last year of high school. Then, suddenly, things turned serious."

"I met Carl at a roller rink in Portland, so I hadn't known him forever, but things still went pretty fast." She thought about the motorcycle ride but decided not to tell Leighton about that.

"You kinda know when that someone is special, don't you?"

Alice nodded. "Yes, I believe you do." She touched his hand. "But your marriage didn't last?" Leighton had mentioned Nancy a few times but always changed the subject. She didn't want to press him now.

"It was because of Hannah. Or so I thought at the time."

"Hannah's cystic fibrosis?"

"Yes. I couldn't see us putting her in a home. That's what Nancy wanted to do. 'We can't raise her with four healthy boys,' Nancy said." He looked away. "I thought it was the very thing Hannah needed. To be around boys who were rambunctious and healthy."

"And she lived longer than some CF kids."

"Yes. And we tried different medications. It was our love that kept her going. I'm convinced of it."

Alice wanted to ask about Aaron but knew Leighton had no clue about his whereabouts. She decided one serious subject was enough for now.

Leighton pulled up into a nursery with a house on the bay. "This is my cousin's, and he said he had some rhodies I could plant."

After a brief introduction of Alice and his cousin, Leighton put the shrubs in the back of the truck and headed out again.

"I suppose you know everyone who lives here."

"Only those who've lived here over twenty years." He met her gaze, then both looked away.

"It's a good place to live, Alice. It was a good place to raise my boys and Hannah."

"The suburbs were good, too."

Leighton nodded. "I hope you don't mind, and I should have asked sooner, but is it okay if we have dinner with Luke and his family and Tom and his wife and kid?"

Alice paused. "I think that would be nice. I'd like to meet your sons."

"Good. Now that that's out of the way, we can relax and have a good time."

fifteen

Leighton chose the 42nd Street Café for dinner. "It's Luke's favorite, and it's closer to Tom's place. He has a summer job painting boats."

"Bet that keeps him busy."

"He likes it because it's close to home and he gets taken out on various boats during the salmon season."

The café was a cottage-style building painted aqua with a deeper aqua trim. The side yard was filled with white Shasta daisies and tall, slender pink hollyhocks. Alice marveled at the sight. The plants seemed more vibrant in color than they did at home.

"I kind of wish I'd at least met Luke at the cannery. Now I have two sons to meet."

He took her hand and led her inside. Bob, the owner, manager, and sometimes cook, ushered them in.

"How's the oyster business doing?" He looked expectantly at Leighton.

"Just fine. Took orders for restaurants in the Portland area, and I guess it's time to get you on the bandwagon also. This is Alice Adams. She's a friend visiting from Portland."

Bob smiled. "Happy to meet you. Hope you enjoy your dinner tonight." He pointed. "Our specials are written on the board in the front."

"We need a large table, enough for nine."

Bob shook his head. "I don't think so. Your son called, saying Lisa isn't feeling well, so the kids are staying home."

"And I wanted Alice to meet Lisa. Guess it'll just be Luke, Tom, and Mary, then." He turned to Alice. "Lisa's the one who's pregnant."

They were led to a table for six in a far corner. Alice admired the antique furnishings and was humming to a tune she knew from the CD that filled the room with soft music.

The sons and Mary arrived at the same time. Alice held her hand out, taking first Luke's hand, noticing how much he looked like Leighton: tall and broad-shouldered, with a thick thatch of dark hair. Tom was shorter but had the same brown eyes that twinkled as she turned toward him.

"Glad to meet you, Alice."

A small woman with a long braid and a wide smile held out her hand. "I'm Mary. And what brings you to the peninsula?"

Alice felt her cheeks flush. "I met Leighton a few weeks ago—"

"Four weeks ago, to be exact," Leighton finished her sentence. "And where is Bunkie?" He turned to Alice. "That's Tom and Mary's only child. She's a girl, a precocious five."

"She's staying for the week with my mother," Mary said. "I'm sure she'll have a fit when she finds out where we came to eat."

"So, now, what do you think of our little spot?" Tom asked, pushing Mary's seat up.

"I'm enjoying everything immensely."

Leighton held Alice's chair out. "I noticed Bob has the special seafood chowder. That's what I'm getting."

Soon two baskets of bread appeared, corn relish, and "our special marionberry-cranberry preserves," the young waitress said.

The evening was pleasant, the brothers sharing stories about the cannery when they worked there each summer and on weekends during the school year. Alice listened intently, wishing she could have known them then.

"I never liked it, though," Tom said, buttering a second slice of bread. "Man, I like this bread. What does it have in it, Mare? Dill?"

"I think so."

"Mary grows herbs and is making the spices Dad is selling in the store now."

"And I couldn't think of doing anything else," Luke added, putting a dollop of corn relish on his bread plate.

"That's what makes it special. Having someone working who likes the job," Leighton interjected. "It always works out for those who love and serve God."

The waitress took their order. Since salad came during the meal, Alice asked for a small portion, with blue cheese dressing.

"It just comes in one size, ma'am."

"Very well. I'll have the seafood chowder, since Leighton recommended it highly." She figured she might be able to finish a bowl of soup sooner than a full dinner. "What's in it?"

"There are three kinds of seafood in the chowder tonight. Clams, halibut, and salmon."

"You'll like it, Alice. I guarantee it," Leighton said. "If not, you can order something else."

"No, that sounds great."

Luke and Tom ordered steaks, and Mary ordered fried chicken. "It's because I can never get it right. I always get chicken when I eat here."

The salads came, along with cups of coffee for the men and Alice, iced tea for Mary. Alice left half of her salad and left the bread alone, though it looked delicious.

The chowder arrived in a wide soup bowl, with a dash of paprika and crushed parsley flakes.

"So, Papa, when is the due date?" Tom asked his older brother.

"Around Christmas, I'm afraid."

Tom grabbed another slice of bread. "Is this going to be it, or are you trying for a basketball team?"

"Three was supposed to be it," Luke said, his eyes all serious. "But sometimes God has something else in mind."

"Tell her we missed her," Leighton said. "I'll stop by with Alice tomorrow and bring her some flowers."

"Hey, Dad, that'd mean a lot to her."

Alice let Leighton finish her chowder, wondering how he

could eat so much. And the boys ate like they hadn't eaten all day. Mary took her chicken home. She'd only eaten the potatoes and gravy.

"Dessert, anyone?" The waitress came and poured more coffee.

"Not for me," all chorused in unison. Alice couldn't have agreed more.

Once out in the parking lot, Luke and Tom teased Leighton about going to Portland to find a date.

"Yeah, Dad. We have women right here."

Alice felt a sinking sensation. Noticing her discomfort, Leighton took her hand. "Alice is a good friend," he said.

"Well, happy to meet you, Alice." Luke walked toward his car. "And we'll probably see you tomorrow."

Mary leaned over and hugged Alice impulsively. "Don't listen to anything they say," she whispered. "They're both protective of their father. It all has to do with Nancy, of course. They don't want to see him hurt."

Alice nodded. "My Courtney says the very same thing."

"If you get a chance, stop by and see my herb garden."

Leighton hugged Mary and each son, then waved.

"I'm sorry about what Tom said. He was just kidding. He's the practical joker of the family."

"You said I was just a friend," Alice said, looking at his profile as he pulled out onto the highway.

"Was that wrong?"

"Well, no. I guess not." She paused. "I think I'll enjoy vespers tomorrow."

"Ah, I recognize that tactic." He took her hand and squeezed it. "Good old changing the subject."

They laughed as they headed for the boardwalk, hand in hand, to watch the kites and the last bit of daylight escape on the far horizon.

❧

Once back at the bed and breakfast, Alice used her credit card to call Courtney. Maybe she was being silly, but she worried about her and needed reassurance that her daughter was okay.

"Mom! I'm surprised to hear your voice. Is everything all right?"

"Yes, Honey. Things are fine. I'll be taking the four P.M. shuttle back tomorrow. Leighton wants me to attend the vespers at three, then I'm off."

"Are you having a good time?"

"A wonderful time."

"And?"

"And what?"

"Is this going to be a monthly occurrence? You go to the beach, then Mr. Walker comes to Portland once a month?"

Alice's heart pounded. She wondered if seeing each other twice a month would be enough, yet he'd said she was just a friend.

"Oh, nothing like that," she finally answered. "We're just friends, that's all."

"Mom, I don't believe that and neither do you."

"But, tell me, how are you doing?"

"I'm fine. Feeling more twinges in my back, but the doctor says that's normal for the second trimester. He said perhaps I should rest more often."

"You're sure you're all right? Did the doctor suggest another ultrasound?

"Those things are expensive. I'm sure I'm doing what all pregnant women do, so stop worrying."

Alice always had worried. Carl used to give her a bad time about it. "Stop worrying, Honey," he'd say. "If God cares for the tiny sparrow, one of the smallest of birds, think of how much He cares for you."

He was right. She always knew that, yet doubts sometimes came in, and worry replaced good common sense.

"I'll see you at evening service then, okay?"

"Sure thing."

Alice held on to the phone after Courtney's good-bye. She

couldn't put her finger on it, but something wasn't quite right. Courtney's voice didn't have the usual lilt. Was she just tired, or had she and Steven had an argument? Courtney usually gave in because it was far easier to do so. She never had liked confrontations. Or could she be concerned about Alice's relationship with Leighton?

Alice sat on the edge of the bed and slipped out of her shoes. She was glad for the phone in her room, as it afforded privacy.

She felt exhausted, then going through all the happenings of the day, knew why. It wasn't as if she were a kid and could bounce back after two hikes and meeting new people and putting a smile on her face constantly. At least here, in the sanctity of her room, she could be herself.

A tap sounded on the door.

"Alice? I have a bit of refreshment for you." Trudy opened the door and entered with a small tray, which held a small pot of tea, two slices of biscotti, and a tiny dish of blackberry preserves.

"The blackberries grow wild here. We're surrounded by bushes. And I don't let any of my guests go hungry. By the way, I understand you like spiced apple tea."

Alice looked startled, then laughed. "That Leighton. Of course he told you!"

Trudy nodded. "That he did."

"As for going hungry, I know that's impossible here. Leighton and his sons eat like loggers."

"It's the salt air, Dear. It gives you an appetite."

"Well, I may have a cup of tea and try one piece of biscotti, but I'm still full from my seafood chowder."

"There's a game of Scattergories in the parlor—if you're interested."

Alice brightened for a moment. "I love the game, but I need time alone. To reflect and write in my journal. Read a few Scriptures."

"I thought so. You do look tired." Trudy paused in the

doorway. "I thought you might like to talk, but I can see you just need peace and quiet. We still have tomorrow."

"Yes, we still have tomorrow," Alice said as she poured the mint-scented tea into a delicate china cup. "Or, as Leighton said earlier, 'Tomorrow is another day.' "

But after Trudy left, Alice wondered what her hostess might want to talk about. Was it something about Leighton, something that would concern her? Maybe she should have acted more interested. Now she'd wonder about it all night.

sixteen

The day had been full, and Leighton came home to rest up, to listen to his messages, to try to figure out what was happening to him. Alice, like a child, loved everything he showed her, every place they went. She was better at hiking than he was, though he hated to admit he was out of shape. He'd been having a problem with arthritis this past year, and it had bothered him when they climbed the hill to Cape D.

Alice had loved the finger sandwiches, fruit, and home-baked cookies Trudy had packed, and they'd enjoyed the surfers at Waikiki Beach. Meeting Luke and Tom for dinner had also gone well, until Leighton kiddingly said something about Alice being just a friend. Her conversation seemed clipped after that.

The answering machine held one message. It was Luke, saying he had two things to discuss.

Leighton grabbed a glass of ice water and sat on the love seat in front of the window before dialing. After they exchanged greetings, Luke got right to the point. "Dad, are you sure you want to get involved with someone who lives so far away?"

Leighton felt his heart soar at the mention of Alice. Of course, Luke would be concerned. It made Leighton feel good that his son cared enough to protest. At least he wasn't being ignored.

"Did you like her?" Leighton said, deliberately not answering the question.

"She seems fine. Kind of quiet."

"Well, what can you expect with you two bazookas talking most of the time?"

"Aw, Dad, I only see Tom once in a blue moon."

"I know."

"Anyway, I realize this person is not just a friend. I saw the way you looked at her when she wasn't looking and the way she looked back when she thought you weren't looking."

"Don't be ridiculous."

"It's never too late to fall in love."

Leighton cleared his throat. "And what was the second concern?"

"Whether we ship oysters to that place in Summersville. They haven't paid for the last shipment."

After discussing that problem, Leighton said he really had to go.

"I'm not letting this issue rest," was Luke's parting remark.

The sun had left the hills, and the room suddenly felt chilly. The house was big, too big for just Leighton. Cora enjoyed keeping it up, and he knew if he had said the word years ago, she would have moved in lock, stock, and barrel. But he couldn't marry for the sake of convenience. There had to be more to a relationship than that. Cora was beautiful. She had a glow about her at times that made him notice her, and once he had thought she might be the one. But she was also stubborn and a bit bossy. He knew if they married, she would run the business and the house and tell him what shirt to wear and how much sugar he could put in his coffee. He didn't want that. He rather liked being his own boss and had decided to keep it that way.

But then Alice had entered his mind—no—make that his heart. He hadn't wanted to let her in, but somehow she had come in, anyway. And now he didn't know if he could let it go any further. He didn't think she felt about him in that way, so why even be concerned about it? Besides, could two people their age really find happiness? At fifty-three, he knew he was set in his ways. He wanted things to keep on just as they had been. Why rock the boat, as the saying went?

He wondered what it would be like to come home to find her in the kitchen, rustling up dinner. Yet even as he thought it, he knew she was closely entwined with her daughter and son-in-law in Portland. He'd heard about one sister she only saw once a week. But Courtney was her whole life. And now there would be a baby. How could he expect her to give that up to move to far-off Oysterville? Even if she loved him, he couldn't ask it of her.

His heart sank at the thought of not seeing her. No, they would just be friends. Friends saw each other often. He could go into Portland more often than in the past. Or would it be easier to let it drop?

Leighton went to his recliner and sat back. He turned the TV on to catch the late news. There was something soothing about watching the news. With all the drive-by shootings, murders, and tornadoes going on, it made a person's problems seem small, by comparison.

He closed his eyes and prayed that he would be content to go on with his life as it had been. There was nothing wrong with that, now, was there?

&

Alice awoke feeling refreshed. It was an overcast day, a layer of clouds shutting out the sun. The smell of coffee had awakened her, but this time she wanted to go downstairs and offer her help.

"Did you have a pleasant sleep?" Trudy smiled as she adjusted a doily on the small table in the foyer. It held a vase filled with wildflowers from the nearby woods.

"It was perfectly wonderful. I needed that sleep."

"Tell me about your day yesterday."

Alice followed Trudy into the kitchen. "Where do I start? Thanks so much for the delicious lunch. We ate it while sitting on piles of driftwood at Waikiki Beach. We came back there after our hike."

"A nice spot, for sure, especially when the sun's out."

"Kids were playing in the water, digging in the sand, and we just sat and watched."

"Come on in and have a cup of coffee with me." Trudy

motioned to a tall stool. "I'm mixing scones for breakfast and need some company. Sometimes I miss women's chatter."

The spacious kitchen, like everything else in the bed and breakfast, was tastefully decorated in shades of green and pink.

"This is such a lovely spot. I'm sure I'll be back."

"Perhaps you'll be back but not staying here. I predict you'll be the lady of the house out on 324th Place."

Alice's cheeks reddened. "Oh, I don't think so. If anyone is the lady of the house, it will be Cora."

Trudy looked up, flour on her hands. "If that were meant to be, Cora would be safely ensconced in the house now. Leighton has been lonely, but even he won't admit it. Cora has kept his house and made him think he's making it just fine alone, but what man doesn't want to find someone to share his life with?"

Alice sipped her coffee, mulling the words over in her mind. "I don't think Leighton is ready to let go of the past."

"You mean Nancy or Cora?" Trudy shook her head. "My dear, Nancy caused him more pain and grief than any two women could. I think what he needs more than anything is to forget Nancy and go on with his life."

"She took her own life."

Trudy nodded. "Yes, but she wasn't in her right mind. I don't know when or why or what happened, but she went from a capricious little thing, so full of life and happy, to a woman who was totally depressed. I think she was under medication in Seattle, but as people often do, I think she went off the meds."

"And she's buried there. Leighton told me that."

"Yes, even though her family has a plot in Lone Fir."

"Is that where Hannah is buried?" Alice had wondered at the time, but sensed that Leighton was uncomfortable talking about his child.

"Hannah is in the Oysterville Cemetery. There was somewhat of a heated discussion about whether she would be buried at Lone Fir with her mother's relatives or in Leighton's family plot. He won, which is at it should be. I can't imagine her family raising such a ruckus, when Nancy treated Hannah that way."

"As you said, Nancy couldn't have been in her right mind. A mother protects her child. She loves and nurtures it, just like a mama bear."

Trudy set the scones aside and pulled a chair out. "I want Leighton to be happy. I think you're the one."

"But we're just friends, Trudy. I admit I have strong feelings for him, but it's way too soon to guess what might happen. Way too soon to speculate on what would be good for him. Or me."

"And you're from the city."

"All my life. And I have my daughter and a dear son-in-law, and a sister who is alone, just as I am. She's been widowed lots longer than me. And there's my church, my volunteer activities; but most of all my only child, Courtney, is expecting a child now."

"I understand. But there are volunteer opportunities here. Portland is less than a three-hour drive away, and if you could find happiness for yourself, don't you think you'd want that? And don't you think your daughter would want that for you also?"

Alice felt excited at the prospect, but she also felt apprehensive. She couldn't even let herself consider it. Besides, there was Cora. Even though Trudy said she wasn't a worry, Cora was ready to fight, if necessary.

"Tell me about Aaron."

Trudy poured two more cups of coffee. "He's another burr under Leighton's saddle. Heaven knows, the man's had enough. Sick child, crazy wife, and a runaway teen."

"Has he tried to find him?"

"Hon, I can talk about Cora or Nancy, but when it comes to Aaron, I just don't know what happened or if Leighton's tried to find him. He's very closemouthed about it. All I remember is that Aaron was the sweetest, kindest kid you'd ever hope to meet. He was so good with Hannah. I think he knew she was dying and couldn't hang around and watch it happen."

"It must have been awful for Leighton."

"The worst thing ever is to lose a child."

"Yes," Alice murmured. "I lost more than one."

The front door opened, and Leighton called out, "Anyone up yet?"

As Alice turned and caught sight of him in the entrance of the kitchen, her heart jumped, and she knew, *knew* in that minute that she wasn't falling in love with this man. He already had her whole heart—hook, line, and sinker.

seventeen

"Hey, you two, since the others aren't up yet, why don't you take your coffee and go in the sunroom?" Trudy pointed to a room with windows facing south and east. Filled with plants of various sizes, it looked like a jungle. Two easy chairs faced the bay.

"Why are you up so early?" Alice asked Leighton as she followed him, coffee in hand.

He grinned. "I might ask you the same thing."

She sat in the paisley-covered wing chair, while he took the burgundy one. "I had a good night's sleep, yet more restless than the night before."

"Why is that?"

"I talked to Courtney right after you left. Says she's fine, yet I have this gut feeling that something is wrong."

"Maybe she's just missing you."

Alice set her cup down. "I suppose that could be. We're close. We've been separated only twice: when she went off to summer camp and when she went east in search of her birth mother."

"And she found her mother?"

"She found most of her family, but her mother had died young. At least, Courtney found her grave and took flowers there."

"That must have been tough."

"Yes, rather traumatic. But she came back with her mother's diary, photos, and a few pictures she had painted in school." Alice remembered how she'd felt when hearing the news. She'd hurt for her daughter, felt hurt that she would never know her mother.

"How long ago was this?"

"Just a year. Right after she met Steven. That's why it was important. She felt she needed to know her medical history before she could marry."

"No skeletons in the closet?"

Alice winced. "Well, I wouldn't say that. Her mother had epilepsy, and her father wouldn't take her to the doctor. He thought she had evil spirits. I don't know the whole story, but Courtney heard all she needed. Steven agreed there were no guarantees when carrying a child. And so they married."

"It's like with Hannah. We had no idea we'd have a sick child, especially not after four healthy boys. But there it was. Cystic fibrosis hits Germans more than any other race."

Leaning over, Alice touched his arm. "I'm sorry for your loss."

"Life goes on. About the search. How did Courtney manage to find her mother?"

"A people locator web site on the Internet couldn't help, but that's because the birth hadn't been recorded. I suggested she go to the town in Illinois where we'd adopted her. She went from town to town and finally found someone who would talk."

"At least she knew where to begin."

"Yes, that helped."

"With Aaron, which I've been wanting to talk to you about, I have no idea where to start searching."

"Courtney might have some ideas. Haven't you tried to locate your son in the past?"

Leighton strode over to the window. How could he explain? In the beginning, he'd tried to find Aaron, but when Hannah turned worse, he'd concentrated on her health. Still, a part of him was missing, and he doubted he would ever feel whole until Aaron was found.

Alice came and stood beside him, slipping her hand into his. "I'm sure it's difficult to talk about. Not knowing is far worse than knowing."

"It's different for men," he finally said. "It isn't that we don't love our children, but we tend to treat sons different. Heaven knows how much I loved Aaron. He was just a happy-go-lucky kid and kept everyone laughing with his antics. Then he changed. Became sullen. Started skipping classes. I didn't know how to handle him and came down hard. Grounded him. He resented it and ran off. He was eighteen."

"Did you look for him then?"

Leighton looked away. "I thought he'd be back."

"I don't see it as any different with a boy," Alice interjected. "Mothers are fiercely protective. Don't come near my child. Don't hurt my child. Fathers are there, but it's just not the same. We try to make them tough so they can go out and face the world. And that's what Aaron decided to do."

"I don't agree about fathers. Men put up this barrier, daring someone to break through, but down deep they're tender-hearted. Just like you. You're hurting far more than you let on."

"Yeah, that might be so. Still—"

"Still, what? A lost child is lost whether it's a boy or girl." She reached up and touched a lock of hair that had a mind of its own. He turned and took her into his arms and held her close. He liked the way her heart sounded against his chest, making him feel alive as old feelings came to the surface, feelings he'd kept deep inside, afraid to let out. Always there was the risk of being hurt. She let herself bask in the comfort of his arms, not wanting the moment to end. He moved away first.

"You've made me think about things, Alice. I know I must find Aaron. It's been too long, and I'm tired of waiting, hoping he'll come back on his own."

"It's good you've come to this decision. And if Courtney can help, I'm sure she'd be happy to."

Voices sounded on the stairway, and seconds later Trudy rang the breakfast bell.

The meal was scrumptious—scones with thick raspberry sauce, a fruit platter, and bacon and ham. A new couple had arrived the night before and sat on one side of the long oak table. Two elderly sisters chatted about the array of food.

At the end of the table closest to the kitchen, Leighton held a chair out for Alice.

"Here is my main dish for the morning!" Trudy proclaimed. "A sausage, asparagus, potato, and cheese medley. I hope you'll like it."

As Trudy cut huge squares, fragrant steam rose from the dish. Soon everyone had a helping. Alice looked across the table at Leighton and felt the color rise to her cheeks.

The sisters introduced themselves as Mattie and Geraldine.

"We feel out of place," Geraldine said. "Here's Cheryl and Ian on their honeymoon, and it's quite obvious from your faces"—she looked from Alice to Leighton—"that if you're not on a honeymoon, you should be!"

Alice blushed deeper. "We're just good friends."

"We've only known each other a few weeks or so," Leighton added.

"My first husband knew me one day before he proposed," Mattie, the younger woman, said. "I was sixteen, isn't that right, Sister?"

The smaller woman nodded while her sister went on. "Geraldine never married because Papa didn't like her intended, so here she is. I say if you find the right person, you should marry. Even if you have to run off."

Mattie, who monopolized the conversation, turned to Leighton. "It's time you started a new life, young man. I don't believe in fortune-telling, but I can tell things by looking at a person's face. You have a good, thoughtful one."

Now it was Leighton's turn to blush.

"I concur," Cheryl, the younger woman, said. "Good advice, Mattie. Life is too short not to go for what you really want."

"And what God deems is important," Trudy added, pouring everyone more coffee. "I ask God what He wants and expects from me each day, and usually I get an answer." She smiled at her guests. "This bed and breakfast came about because of an answer to prayer, a prayer that I'd find something new and a way to be useful in my remaining years."

They all clapped. "And a great answer to prayer," Alice said. "I've never stayed in a bed and breakfast, and I like the idea. You get to know people from all over."

"Now, if you'll excuse me, I must pack." She hurried up the stairs to gather her belongings. They wouldn't return to Trudy's before Alice had to leave on the Bay Shuttle.

When Alice came back downstairs, Trudy had another picnic basket ready. "You have so much to do. Enjoy this before the vespers service."

The first stop was the cannery and Leighton's new store with gift items. Customers could also order fresh oysters. Alice bought two jars of spice and a can of smoked oysters. "For Steven. The spices are for Courtney."

"Good choice," the lady behind the counter said.

Leighton opened a door and motioned Alice to go ahead of him. "Goodness, but there are hundreds of them," Alice said, watching four workers standing over stainless steel bins while they sorted mounds of oysters.

In a small office off to one side, Luke looked up from a desk. He nodded. "Hello again," he said, as Leighton and Alice entered.

Amazed, she continued to watch the workers through an office window. "These oysters are shipped across the bay. There they're opened and sent back to us," Luke explained.

"We're not a full-fledged cannery, though I always refer to it as one," Leighton said. "But the bay is a good place to produce oysters, and they're in high demand, as I'm sure you know."

Alice followed Leighton through a back door. They looked out over the bay. The tide was out now, leaving mudflats nearly as far as she could see.

"Can we walk on the mudflats?" Alice asked.

"Not unless you have boots. It looks solid, but the ground is swampy."

"Who's that man walking out there, then?"

"That's old Charlie. He walks every day on the flats. Not

sure why. It's just what he does."

Charlie looked up and waved. Leighton waved back.

Luke came out. "Lisa was disappointed she didn't get to meet you. Next time, we'll have you over for dinner."

Next time. It was as if he expected her to return. After last night, Alice thought Leighton's sons didn't like her.

She smiled. "I hope Lisa's feeling better soon. I'd love to meet your family."

A gentle breeze blew in from the bay, and Leighton put an arm around her. "Should I get your sweater from the truck?"

"I'm fine."

They headed to Leadbetter Point. Leighton parked the truck in a shady area, and mosquitoes buzzed around them in droves. Leighton withdrew a bottle of insect repellant from the glove compartment. "Lots more of these insects where we're going."

"Is it far?"

"Two miles to the ocean side and two back, unless we get lost."

"Leighton, you wouldn't get lost."

"It's been known to happen. I think there are a couple of people from Seattle still out there somewhere, wandering around. We just might run into them."

She hit his arm playfully and proceeded down the well-marked trail.

When they got to the ocean side, Alice ran onto the beach, exclaiming over the sand dollars. "I must take some home. They're beautiful." She held one up and let the sand pour out.

"I just happen to have a plastic bag in my pocket."

Alice looked at him, shaking her head. "You think of everything. Of course, you knew there'd be sand dollars here, didn't you?"

"Yes, I did. And I also knew you'd want to gather some."

Soon the bag was full of whole sand dollars, and Leighton led the way back. "Be sure to look for any signs of those missing people."

"Yeah, sure."

When they got to the truck, he took out a blanket and led the way down to the bay side. "I know the perfect spot for our picnic."

Fried chicken, potato salad, jam bars, and small cans of apple juice were in the basket. "A regular feast. Trudy thinks of everything," Alice said, taking a napkin after she'd finished eating. "That was delicious."

Leighton leaned over and wiped a smudge of jam from her cheek.

"It's time to go to vespers."

The service was wonderful. Alice loved the old church with its high ceilings and flowered wallpaper, listening to the matriarch of Oysterville giving the history of the church and area. The old pump organ had a unique sound, and Alice and Leighton shared a hymnal while they sang "Stand Up, Stand Up for Jesus."

Leighton leaned over and took her hand. "This is the last time we'll be together for a while," he whispered.

"I know."

"Unless I come back to Portland."

"Which you will," Alice said with a half smile.

When they stepped out into the afternoon, warm light had broken through the clouds. "It's sunny, now that I'm leaving to go home," Alice said.

"Speaking of which, there's Mel now."

Leighton retrieved Alice's bags from his truck, stowing them in the back of the van. He leaned over and kissed her forehead. "I'll send you a card. It'll be waiting when you get home."

She wished he were going with her now. Wished she didn't have to leave yet knew she must. He waved until the van turned the corner onto Sandridge Road.

"So? How do you like our peninsula?" Mel asked.

"I like it very much." She sighed. "Leighton's a wonderful person, isn't he?"

"The best. He cares about the community and gives far more than people realize. He also treats employees fairly."

"That doesn't surprise me." Alice already knew it didn't take much to love the tall, lean man.

"You'll be back," Mel predicted.

"Perhaps."

"No, you will. I'd bet on it."

She wanted to ask him about Cora but decided against it. She didn't want to gossip behind Leighton's back. It didn't seem right.

When Mel pulled into the driveway nearly three hours later, Alice expected to see Steven's car. It was almost time for the evening service. Even when they didn't come for dinner, they drove to pick her up.

"Just a minute, Mel. Will you wait until I check to see if everything is all right?"

Mel had her two bags and headed up the walkway. "You want to check in the house?"

She nodded as she unlocked the door. "I'm one of those people who are scared to go into an empty house after I've been gone. It's especially scary at night."

"I'll look in the closets and under the beds."

Alice could see he thought it was a laughing matter, but he humored her. She heard doors open and close. Then he was back. "Looks okay."

"I've been afraid since I was a child. Carl tried to talk me out of it, and I was okay for a while." She had looked under all the beds now. "After he died, I was worse than before."

The light blinked on the answering machine. She handed Mel a tip and thanked him for coming in to check things out.

"I'll be on my way now," he said.

"Thanks again, Mel."

"That's okay. I'd do anything for Leighton."

Alice closed the door and rushed to the phone. She hit the machine's playback button. Steven's voice cut through the stillness of the house. "Alice, we're not going to the evening service. Courtney's tired. She's okay, so don't worry. Call us when you get in. And I repeat, *don't worry*."

Alice's fingers shook as she dialed the number. Courtney's voice answered right away. "Mom? I'm so glad you're home."

"I should come over right now."

"No, that isn't necessary. I'm okay. I just had a bad night; I think it was gastritis. I knew I shouldn't have eaten that Italian sausage and spaghetti yesterday."

"Sweetie, are you sure?" Alice thought back to when she miscarried, but it had always been in the first trimester. Courtney was far past that. "Are you sure you shouldn't go to the emergency room tonight?"

"No. I'm okay. I need to rest and didn't think it would be good to try to go to the evening service. I'm dying to hear all about the trip, so will I see you tomorrow?"

"You're sure you don't want to go in and be checked?"

"No. I'll call tomorrow if I still have the pain."

After unpacking a few things, but not all, Alice turned on her computer to check her E-mail. She had not one, but two messages from Leighton.

She clicked on the first one.

> *I'm so glad you came to my corner of the world. I hope you had a good time. Luke and I were talking about you again. Seems you are my favorite topic of discussion. I miss you already.*
>
> > *Leighton*

The second one was a card, but she didn't want to look at it just yet. She hit the respond button and poured out her heart and worries to him.

> *My daughter is having abdominal pains. Remember when I said I didn't think her voice sounded right? I'm really worried. Thanks for the great time. I miss you already, too.*
>
> > *Love,*
> > *Alice*

Leighton never used the word *love,* and Alice thought it strange. It was as if he didn't like the word, as if it scared him. Perhaps she used it too randomly.

She hit the send button, then returned to finish emptying her suitcase. The phone rang. Grabbing it, she almost yelled a hello.

"Alice?"

"Leighton! I just read your message. You didn't get my answer already?"

"No. I just wanted to hear your voice. What is it? Is something wrong?"

She swallowed back the tears that suddenly threatened. "It's Courtney. She's having abdominal pains. I'm so afraid for her and the baby."

"Do you want me to come?"

"Oh, no. It's okay. I know you're busy."

"I'll come if you want me to. You shouldn't be alone when you're upset."

"No. Just keep in touch, okay?"

She hung up and the tears ran down her cheeks. She wanted him to come, wanted him to be there. She needed someone to lean on, to assure her that things would work out. If only she could stop worrying, stop thinking the worst would happen. Carl had always chided her for jumping to conclusions.

Hurrying to the kitchen, Alice put the teakettle on. Perhaps a cup of tea would soothe her.

Then she saw the roses on the dining room table. Their petals drooped a bit, but the stems still stood straight and tall. Tears sprang again to her eyes. She thought of God and how He was there to lean on.

"O Lord, please hear me now. My little girl's in trouble. Don't let anything happen to her baby, I beg of You."

She sat with her head bowed, one pink rosebud clutched in her hand.

eighteen

Alice slept with the light on all night, something she did when worried. Light offered her comfort, just like the Bible on her nightstand. She thought of one of the first verses she had memorized: "Thy word is a lamp unto my feet, and a light unto my path."

She remembered going to Sunday school in a starched dress, knee highs, and black patent leathers. Agnes balked about going after she turned thirteen, but Alice accepted Christ as her personal Savior at a young age and attended the youth group and all other activities. She missed her parents now, wishing they had lived long enough to see Courtney marry.

Alice wondered if it was too early to call Courtney. She'd have a cup of coffee then call.

No answer. Alice sank against the pillow. Courtney had gone to the hospital during the night, and Steven hadn't called her. She was sure that's what had happened. She dialed Steven's cell phone.

"Steven, where's Courtney?"

There was a long pause. "At home, I assume. I left less than an hour ago. She didn't answer the phone?"

"No. That's why I called you."

"She's probably in the shower. Try again. If she doesn't answer this time, I'll go home to check things out."

She dialed again and Courtney answered. "Mom, I just got your frantic message. I'm sorry. Steven says I should take the phone into the bathroom."

"Honey, I was scared to death."

"I'm going in to see the doctor tomorrow because he's not going to be in the office today. But I feel fine now. No pains. I'm a little tired, that's all."

"Oh, praise God." Alice felt she could breathe again. "If you're feeling up to it, let's go see Agnes this afternoon."

"That's a great idea. I want to hear about Oysterville and all the things you saw."

Alice checked her E-mail before calling Agnes.

"Of course I want to see you," Agnes said. "Come for lunch. I missed the two of you yesterday. Just didn't seem like Sunday. And what's this about your going somewhere to see a man?"

Alice chuckled. "I'll tell you about it when we get there."

When Courtney was in the car, Alice studied her critically. "You look peaked."

Courtney adjusted the seat belt to accommodate her expanding tummy. "Mom, I'm fine. If I weren't, I wouldn't be going with you."

"Agnes is going to give me the third degree about Leighton."

"Of course she is. Isn't that what big sisters are for?"

"Exactly what did you tell her?"

Courtney grinned. "That I thought you were serious about this guy. Why else would you have gone all that way to visit?"

"Well, we'll deal with the topic, should it come up."

The subject came up after hugs and hellos.

"I can't wait to hear the news," Agnes said, "but since the soup's hot and the sandwiches toasted, let's eat." They always had the same meal. It was tradition.

As soon as they sat and offered a blessing, Agnes started in. "Please tell me you're not seriously considering remarriage at your age!"

"You think I shouldn't?" Not that Alice was contemplating it, but she wanted to see Agnes's reaction.

"What I think doesn't matter, but you're crazy, that's what! One doesn't go running off to who knows where on a whim. I know you too well."

Alice stirred her soup. "I distinctly remember you telling me once that I should think of marrying again."

"Well, I meant someone from your church, not some guy

from another state."

"Oysterville's just one hundred and fifty miles away."

Agnes hadn't had a happy marriage. After her husband's death, she never considered dating again, let alone marrying. But she thought male companionship might be good for Alice, who seemed far more dependent and was lost without Carl.

Alice expected Courtney to join in the conversation, but she remained silent.

"It's way too far, considering your family is here." Agnes set a plate of shortbread cookies on the table.

Alice chewed on her toasted cheese as she tried to gather her thoughts. Agnes had been the forceful one, the one who got her way. Though she and Alice saw each other once a week, Agnes always sat like a queen on her throne, expecting her dictate to be met.

"Leighton is a very fine man, Auntie," Courtney finally said. "You should come to meet him. He brought Mom pink roses."

"Roses! Do you know how much they cost now?"

Alice nodded. "Courtney's right. He is very thoughtful— all the things you'd ever want in a man—"

"Hold on." Agnes raised her hand. "Just what are these attributes? Maybe we should make a list."

"Security," Courtney said.

"He's a Christian, and he's compassionate."

"How do you know that?" Agnes asked. "Seems you haven't known him long enough to have that one figured out."

"Companionship," Courtney said. She'd often mentioned how much she and Steven enjoyed being together and felt free to talk about anything.

"He's nice-looking, though I don't count that as a must," Alice said.

"But he's taking you away."

"Oh, Agnes, we haven't even discussed that yet."

"If his job is on the bay, growing oysters and selling them, why does he come to Portland?"

Alice nibbled a cookie. "He has a son and business here

also." She suddenly remembered he had another order, and knowing how she had worried so much, he'd probably be back sometime this week. Her face got red. She needed to change the subject.

Alice leaned toward Courtney. "So, Agnes, what do you think of our girl here? Doesn't she look radiant? And she's really showing now."

Courtney pulled her jumper close to reveal the baby. "Six months, Auntie."

"And it's a boy?"

Courtney nodded. "Steven Carl."

"Steven Carl!" Alice cried. "I didn't know you'd picked out a name."

"We did. Just last night."

"I like it. After Daddy and Granddaddy." Agnes turned to Alice.

"And you're going to just leave, with the baby coming."

"Agnes, I am *not* leaving."

"Humph! I think you will."

Courtney went over and hugged her aunt. "Everything will work out, but we need to go now. It's been wonderful as always, Auntie."

Agnes stood in the doorway, waving, her body erect, her face dispassionate.

"Maybe Auntie is jealous." Courtney looked at her mother.

"I wondered about that. Visits with Agnes wear me out. She's too argumentative and looks for something to complain about. She wasn't always that way. We had fun when we were kids."

"Perhaps she wants to remarry, though she says she doesn't want to."

"She'll never meet anyone stuck in her apartment day in and day out," Alice said.

"Well, I say let's take it a day at a time. No sense in making hay if there's no grass in the yard."

Alice laughed. "I never heard that one!"

Courtney smiled impishly. "I just made it up."

"I love you; you do know that."

"Of course."

"And Steven's a lucky man."

"He knows that." Courtney stuck her chin up then grinned. "I'm lucky to have him, too."

They drove along I-84 and Alice took the 82nd St. Exit. "Do you want to go home or stop by the house?"

"Let's stop at your house first," Courtney answered. "I think I'll lie down for a nap, if that's okay."

Alice frowned. "You sure you feel all right?"

"Yes. It's just that I need more rest now." She leaned back against the headrest.

"Of course. And I'll check my E-mail."

"Mom, you're fanatical. I can't believe it!"

"Yeah, you've got that one right."

There were two messages. The first was from Leighton, saying he might be in town on Wednesday.

"Wednesday," Alice said aloud. "That's the day after tomorrow."

The second letter was from an unknown address. The message was chilling. "You don't know what you're doing or who you are fooling with." It was unsigned.

Alice felt sudden fear. Who would send such a message? It must just be some sick joke. Why would anyone wish her harm? She hadn't done anything to anyone. She thought of Cora. But, no, it couldn't be her. Even Cora wouldn't do something like that.

She jotted down the address from the letter, and after reading Leighton's message again, she printed it out.

Courtney was still napping, so Alice called Steven and asked him to come by for dinner.

"I'll be there no later than six."

She told him about the message.

"Alice, don't open any letter unless it's from a known address."

"I didn't know that."

"There're a lot of crazies out there, so just be aware. Leave the message alone, and I'll take a look at it."

Alice left the computer on and went in to make an apple pie, Steven's favorite. It was the least she could do for all his help with the computer.

Steven looked perplexed when he came into the kitchen. "Do you know a Meredith?"

"Meredith? No, should I?"

"I found a name from the server, but they can't tell me any-more. I sent a message, saying we'd call the police if there was any more harassment."

"Harassment! One letter is hardly that, is it, Steven?" She quartered the apple, wondering who Meredith could be. She certainly hadn't met anyone named Meredith.

"Maybe it isn't harassment, Alice, but you can't be too careful." He looked at the apples in a bowl. "Are you making an apple pie, by chance?"

"Sure am. Now you must stay for dinner."

"You know how to drive a hard bargain."

Courtney cleared her throat behind them. "Hey, guys, don't I have any say in where I eat?" She grinned impishly. "I'm feeling better now. Sometimes sleep is all a person needs." She patted her tummy. "I just wish he wanted to sleep when I do."

Steven leaned over and kissed his wife. "Honey, you're beautiful right now. I love you so much."

Alice dumped the apples into the crust, wondering how she could even think for one minute that she might be happy living somewhere else. This was home. It would always be home.

nineteen

By mid-September, Leighton had come to Portland at least once a week, and Alice had gone to the peninsula twice a month. Courtney seemed to be fine with no more abdominal pain and was counting the days until her baby came. Now that she was in the final two months of her pregnancy, Alice didn't worry as much.

Courtney had collected every conceivable gadget and piece of furniture from a changing table to baby scales. Blankets, sleepers, socks, and rompers filled the chest of drawers. The Ladies' Guild at church had given a baby shower. Since she needed more space, Courtney found another dresser at a yard sale and was in the process of sanding it down. Steven promised to paint it.

The last time Alice had visited Leighton, they found a delightful baby book at Sweet William's, an exclusive gift boutique in Ocean Park. Courtney loved it on sight as she leafed through the pages.

"It's actually from Leighton," Alice said. "He saw it and insisted on buying it."

"I'll have to write him a thank-you note."

"I'm sure he'd appreciate it."

When they weren't together, Alice and Leighton E-mailed daily. She couldn't imagine life without him and thought he felt the same. Each time it was more difficult to say good-bye, yet nothing was brought up about a permanent relationship. He'd attended church with her more than one Sunday, meeting her friends, and she'd had dinner with Luke and his family. She'd also seen Cora again, and Cora had been cordial.

Each time Alice went to the peninsula, she stayed with Trudy at the bed and breakfast. She'd learned what to wear to the beach now—her warm gray hat with earflaps, jeans, and layers of clothes. Mornings were cool, but afternoons were often warm. It was hard to know what to expect.

Alice and Leighton had hiked on every trail from the south end to the north. He'd started teasing her, calling her a mountain goat.

"I don't mind being a goat," she said. "Suits me just fine."

Alice had come for the Beach Barons' Car Extravaganza.

"You're going to think of me as a permanent fixture," she said when she arrived at Trudy's.

"And that would suit me just fine." The older woman gave her a quick hug. "I enjoy the company."

The night before the car parade, Alice and Trudy sat on the front porch shelling peas.

"I guess I should be content with things the way they are. Why can't I just be happy to have Leighton as a good friend?"

Trudy raised an eyebrow. "You don't think you're more than just a friend?"

"Nothing's been said about making our relationship permanent. It probably wouldn't work, anyway."

"Of course it will," Trudy said.

"I could hardly expect Leighton to move to Portland. His work, his whole life is here."

"And you don't think he wants you to move here?"

"I suppose he does," Alice hesitated, "but I'm not sure I can leave my daughter and grandbaby."

Trudy shook the pea pods out of her lap. "I know I'm old-fashioned, but I say it's the woman's choice. If the man earns a living, she should go where he can make that living. I'm sure Leighton notices hesitancy on your part, and that's why he hasn't suggested marriage."

"He sends the cutest cards. Some are romantic, but he never signs them with love."

Trudy glanced at the road. "As I said before, Leighton's been hurt deeply. He doesn't want to risk another failure or a possible rejection."

"I'd *never* reject him. I know I love him. I knew from the beginning."

"It'll work, then, because I know he loves you, too. He's as much as said so to me."

"And what about Cora?"

"Cora has to find her own happiness. She clung to an idea too long. It's time for her to move on, and I think she's finally come to realize the futility of a life with Leighton."

"I wish we could find Aaron, too. I know how it hurts Leighton."

"Aaron will be found. I have every confidence that he will. It's just a matter of time." Trudy rose from the chair. "Let's go pick some wildflowers for the table and see if there's enough ripe blackberries for a cobbler."

"Are you sure Leighton's coming for dinner?"

"He said he was. Said he had a meeting with Luke, then he'd be right over."

Alice popped a ripe berry into her mouth. She made a face. It looked ripe but was tart.

Trudy laughed. "That's why you have to add lots of sugar. You just never know how many are really sweet."

⋆

Leighton knew what he had to do. It wouldn't be easy, but some decisions weren't. He'd discuss his plan with Luke.

He found Luke overseeing the shipment of oysters. The truck was full. Ken, the driver, nodded. "Hi, Mr. Walker."

Luke held out the shipping ledger for Leighton to read. "What's wrong? I thought you were taking off for the day."

"We need to talk. Can you leave Tim in charge and come with me to get a cup of coffee?"

Luke frowned. Leighton never took off during the day, nor did he suggest coffee in the middle of the afternoon. "Sure, Dad. Whatever you want."

"Can you run this operation without me?"

The question threw Luke off-guard, and he stepped back. "Well, I think so, Dad—"

"No, you have to know. No thinking about it."

"Yes, I know what all you do, and I suppose I always figured someday you'd turn it over to me. I just thought it wouldn't be for another ten years or so."

"I'm putting you in charge now, but first we need to talk. I'll meet you at Jeanine's in ten minutes. I'll ask her for a back room so we can have some privacy."

Jeanine's was not the place he usually went. She made lattés with soy milk and did a lot of natural food stuff that Leighton wasn't into, but she had a large clientele and that suited Leighton's needs. She also made the best smoked turkey sandwich he'd ever tasted. Of course it was too late for lunch, so he and Luke would have to settle for coffee and a piece of her fresh rhubarb pie.

"Hey, how's the oyster business?" she asked when he got there.

"Doing fine, just fine."

"Where's that friend of yours that came in a few weeks ago with you?"

"Alice?"

Jeanine smiled. It was the kind of smile that lit up her whole face. "Yeah, guess that was her name."

"She's here now."

"Oh?" She looked as if she expected him to go on with more details.

"I'm meeting Luke," he said, ignoring her probing question. "Can we have that table in the back where you have the knitting classes?"

"Of course you can. What are you ordering?"

"Two coffees and two slabs of rhubarb pie."

"Just sold the last piece, Leighton. I have coconut cream, though."

"Okay. That'll do." He didn't really care what she had. He just needed to do something with a fork while they talked. Luke had never been easy to talk to. Quiet. Stubborn. He had a touch of his father in him.

Jeanine brought the coffees back just as Luke came in.

"For Pete's sake, Dad," he muttered after she left, "what's going on? We've never come in here for coffee before. This is the sort of place I'd take Lisa to."

"I know."

"So what's up?"

Leighton took a sip of coffee and watched Jeanine set a slice of pie in front of his bewildered son.

"Pie?" Luke said. "Now if you'd said we were coming for pie, that's a whole different thing."

"Shut up and eat," Leighton said. His voice sounded gruff, but his mouth turned up at the ends.

"Okay. I'm waiting."

"I hear you and Cora have been talking about me behind my back."

Luke almost choked on his coffee. "What?"

"She said you two and Tom had discussed my life and all of you agreed I had no business getting interested in a woman who isn't from around here."

"Dad, now, that's not fair."

"What's not fair? That I'm calling you on the carpet about it, or that I found you out?"

"You know what I mean—"

"No, I don't. That's why we're here."

Luke played in the pie with his fork. "It's just that, well, Cora would make you a really good wife, so why look somewhere else?"

Leighton narrowed his eyes. "What if I'd told you that Lisa wasn't right for you? What would you have done?"

"Ignored you, probably." He dug in and polished off his pie in record time, then shoved the plate back. "I know it's none of my business, and it was Cora who brought it up. I just sort of agreed with her."

"Which gave her fuel for her cause." Leighton leaned forward. "Luke, do you believe in love?"

"Ah, Dad, of course I do."

Jeanine reappeared, holding up the coffeepot. "Yeah, refills would be nice," Leighton said. He knew she was wondering what was going on. "Not selling the business, Jeanine. Just want you to know that."

"Oh, good. I'm relieved to hear that." She smiled, then left them alone again.

Leighton picked up the conversation. "If you believe in love, as you say you do, and if you believe things happen for reasons and that God is the Supreme Maker and if we know what's good for us, we ask for His guidance, then you wouldn't agree with Cora. I don't love Cora, I've never loved Cora, and frankly, I doubt I'll *ever* fall in love with her."

"Okay, okay, Dad. Don't get hot under the collar. Keep your voice down. If you don't watch out, she might pop in at any moment. This is one of her favorite places to go, or didn't you know that?"

"No, I didn't. How would I know that?"

Luke downed his coffee and pushed his chair back. "So I said something I shouldn't, and I apologize. I have nothing against Alice, but she's a city gal. You know what happens to city gals. Look what happened to that appliance repairman, Fred, when he married Rachel. He stayed on, but she moved back to Seattle."

"I know that, Son. And that's why I want you to take over the business in my absence."

"Absence!"

"I plan on being gone for a while. I'll keep in touch, and if there are any big problems, you can call me. I'll be just three hours away."

Luke shook his head. "You're not making sense. How can you leave something you've done your entire life? If you'd gone to the city, my mother might be here today—" His voice trailed off, as if realizing he'd said too much.

Leighton looked at his son, feeling the hurt return, the hurt he'd felt when Nancy first left, the hurt when he'd received the news of her death, the hurt when he heard of the note she'd left behind. A note that said she'd be buried in Seattle, not in the family plot on the peninsula.

Luke had also felt this hurt, perhaps more than the younger boys. He'd known his mother the best and had acted up in school for several months after she first left. He'd been old enough to remember the arguments when she'd begged Leighton to "get out of this godforsaken spot and move to Seattle or Portland. Somewhere else, *anywhere else!*"

Leighton tightened his jaw. "You're hitting low, Luke. Mighty low."

"Sorry, Dad. I shouldn't have said that."

"People change over the years. They grow; they learn to listen and to feel with their heart, not just their head. Perhaps that's the crossroads I'm at now. But it isn't going to be forever."

"It isn't?"

"No. I want to be up there for Alice, to be with her while her daughter's going through this pregnancy. It's important to her. She doesn't have a bunch of kids to shuffle through, you know. When you have just one, you look at them with a whole different perspective."

"Dad, I'll run the business. I can manage without you. It may take more time than I'm putting in now, and quite honestly, I don't know how Lisa will take it. But if it isn't forever, she'll understand. Just as I'm trying to understand how you can even leave the peninsula."

The two shook hands, then Leighton watched his son head back toward the cannery. He paid for the coffee and pie and told Jeanine that if she ever stopped baking pies, he'd move away.

He walked out, smelled the wonderful salt air, the clean air, something he would miss in Portland. But he couldn't have everything, could he? Alice needed him now, and he was going to be there for her if the city killed him. It wasn't as if he couldn't get away and come back down for a weekend.

He squared his shoulders, then took one more deep breath before heading to Trudy's.

twenty

Alice returned home with Leighton's words running through her mind. What had he meant when he said things were going to work out? She had begged him to tell her what he was talking about, but he said, no, the time wasn't right. She guessed she'd just have to bide her time, but it wouldn't be easy.

Three days later, Courtney called with exciting news. "Mom, you'll never guess what!"

"You know I'm horrible at guessing games, so just tell me."

"I got a lead on Aaron. I'm calling Leighton immediately, or do you want to?"

"Oh, no, Sweetie. You call him. You did the work. He's going to be beside himself with joy."

"I know. I just hope it pans out."

Courtney located Leighton through his cell phone. "There's an Aaron Walker in East Belfast, Maine."

"You're kidding! You really think it might be him? Do you have a phone number and an address?" Leighton's first thought was to fly to Maine and see Aaron face-to-face.

"No address, just this number."

"I'll take it."

Aaron Matthew. He felt a tight knot in his throat at the thought of his son. Missing. A runaway. Not one of those who heard the 800 number and called home to say, "I'm fine, Dad." No. That wasn't Aaron's way. And here, perhaps, he had been found, but did he want that? Leighton had hoped since that day five years ago when he left, that one day he'd open the door and there would be Aaron. Of course he'd throw his arms around him and call Luke and Tom, then John. There'd be rejoicing, just like with the prodigal son in the Bible. Leighton would want to share that special time with Alice. There was almost too much to think about.

What should he say to a son he hadn't seen for so many years?

Courtney said Aaron was working in a lobster pound in Maine. Who would have thought it? Leighton figured that Aaron would get as far away from the sea as he could. He'd never seemed to like the oyster business or anything about the water.

Leighton finally mustered enough courage to dial the 207 area code then the rest of the number.

He got an answering machine. It wasn't Aaron's voice. Disappointment hit him, but he left a message, anyway.

"This is Leighton Walker, and I'm trying to reach my son, Aaron Walker. If I have the right number, will you please call home? Aaron, I love you."

Leighton didn't leave the house that day. He sat staring out at the bay. He couldn't E-mail Alice because that would tie up the line. Now he wished he had two separate lines as Tom had suggested in the beginning. When he remembered to use his cell phone, she wasn't home.

The phone rang at eight P.M.

"Dad?"

He choked on the sudden tears in his throat. "Son? Is this my Little Buddy?" Buddy had been a childhood pet name for Aaron.

"Yes, this is Little Buddy." Aaron's voice broke. "Dad, we have so much to talk about."

"That we do. Oh, that we do. But just knowing you're alive and well, that's an answer to my most fervent prayer."

"I figured you might not want anything to do with me."

"Oh, Son, I'd never turn you away. A child is never lost to his parent. Never." Alice had helped him see that. She'd said that as long as Aaron was lost, Leighton wouldn't be able to go ahead with his life. He'd never looked at it that way, but she made him see lots of things he hadn't seen before.

"I know that Hannah died."

"It was inevitable." The tears welled up again. "How did you find out?"

"I subscribed to the *Chinook Observer.* I knew they'd have it in there."

Leighton still couldn't believe he was talking to his son after all this time. "Aaron, I have to see you. Can I come there, or should I send money for a flight home?"

"I want to come now, but I'd have to give notice. It wouldn't be fair to leave Mick hanging. He's been good to me and helped me out more than once."

"Yes, Son." Leighton didn't know who Mick was or what he'd done, but he understood an obligation.

"And if I come, it will be because I can afford to. I can't take handouts; I don't deserve it."

"It wouldn't be a handout, Aaron. You're my boy. I want to see you."

"I'll be home by Thanksgiving, okay?"

In the end, Leighton had to agree. "But we can talk to each other?"

"Sure, Dad. Every week, or as often as you want."

As he hung up, Leighton thought of Aaron as a toddler, at age two. Independent. Bullheaded. Here he was still, the captain of his own ship, balking at any suggestion his father made.

Leighton got on his knees and thanked God for answered prayer, for finding that his son was alive and well, but more importantly that he would be coming home in two months.

The next morning Cora called him before he left for work.

"I got word that you found Aaron and he's coming home. How can you just forgive him like that?" she demanded.

"Cora, you always loved Aaron. How can you even think I'd turn my back on him? Surely you remember the story of the prodigal son."

"That's a parable."

"So? Jesus taught with parables. It's one of the most remembered and most cherished parables of all times."

"I don't think it's fair to Luke."

"I don't hear Luke complaining."

"No, you wouldn't. Luke doesn't make his thoughts known all that much."

"You're telling me that Luke is unhappy about Aaron returning to Oysterville?"

"Yes, I am."

"Well, I'll just see about that," Leighton muttered under his breath.

Halfway to work he stopped and parked alongside the road. Cora had done it again. Gotten him hot under the collar and all ready to pounce on Luke, then he remembered what had happened last time.

No way was he going to ask Luke how he felt about it. If Aaron came home, he could help Luke run the business. Having Aaron home would be an asset and certainly not the way Cora made it sound.

He called Alice on the cellular phone, saying he was sending a big bouquet of flowers to Courtney. "What does she like best?"

"Carnations. Any color. She just likes their fragrance."

"Carnations it is, then. I—" He hesitated. "I'll see you soon, I hope."

৵

In the middle of the night, Courtney awoke with a wet, sticky feeling. She groped for the lamp, gasping when she saw the blood. She shook Steven. "It's the baby! I'm losing the baby!"

He rolled over to the edge of the bed. "Honey, no." Anguish spread across her face as she pointed to her nightgown. He reached for the phone. "I'm calling the doctor."

"No, Steven. It's too late for that. Please just—" she gasped for breath—"take me to the hospital."

He found her jumper on the back of a chair, groped for the sandals under the bed, and grabbed a towel. He didn't remember getting dressed or bringing the car out front, but he helped Courtney, who was almost hysterical, into the front seat.

She lay her head back, a grimace crossing her forehead.

"I better call Alice."

"Call from the hospital," she said. "Oh, Steven, this can't be happening!"

Steven sped over the limit toward Providence Hospital. Thank goodness it was only five miles away. He prayed for a policeman to come along, but the streets were deserted. The car clock said two A.M.

"I know this is bad," Courtney whimpered again. "It shouldn't be happening. The baby must be in distress."

"Honey, we're almost there." Steven had called ahead to the hospital, alerting them to the emergency, and they were waiting with a wheelchair at the entrance.

"Steven," Courtney grabbed his arm. "Don't leave me." Her eyes were wide with shock.

"Honey, you know I wouldn't."

She began crying softly then, and by the time she was wheeled into one of the examining rooms and the doctor on duty came to check, she was openly sobbing. The doctor was young, and Steven hoped he knew what he was doing.

"Mrs. Spencer, please try to relax. We're here to help. I think you have a condition called placenta previa. Your chances of keeping the baby are good."

Courtney cried harder. "No, I know it's too late."

"Honey, please." Steven stroked her arm.

"How far along are you?"

"Seven months," Steven answered. He knew as much about the pregnancy as Courtney did. "It's our first."

"Did anything unusual happen today?"

"Oh, no. I take very good care of myself—"

"No previous miscarriages?"

"No."

"She's had a relatively easy time of it," Steven offered.

"Have you had an ultrasound?"

Courtney nodded. "Yes, back at the end of June."

"Everything looked okay then?"

"Yes, everything's been fine all along," Steven interrupted.

His voice was harsh, but he couldn't help it. Why didn't this doctor *do* something?

"Honey, I better call your mother." He took his cell phone and stepped into the hall. Of course, Alice would be asleep, but if he waited until morning, she would be deeply hurt.

Alice answered with a sleepy "Hello?" but instantly came awake. "I'll be right there," she said.

Steven went back in and took Courtney's hand.

"Complete bed rest is a must if you're to keep the baby," the doctor was saying. "I've ordered an ultrasound so we can see how things look. It will show the extent of the condition, since there are various stages."

Courtney's face was pale, and her chin trembled as she looked from the doctor to Steven and back again. "But what happened?"

"It happens in one of two hundred pregnancies. The placenta is covering the cervix and it causes bleeding. Have you had contractions?"

"No."

"We'll know more once we see the ultrasound."

Alice arrived in a taxi, not trusting herself to drive in the middle of the night, especially not when she was upset.

Steven heard her voice in the hall and stepped out to motion her in.

"They've scheduled an ultrasound. Until then, we wait."

Alice bent over Courtney and kissed her cheek. She tried not to cry, but the tears welled up and spilled down her face.

"Honey, I'm so sorry."

"It isn't definite that she's losing the baby," Steven said. "The doctor says the bleeding might stop."

"Mom—" Courtney opened her eyes and reached for her mother's hand.

They were crying when the nurse came in and suggested that Courtney needed her rest. Courtney begged for either Steven or Alice to stay with her.

Steven left to get a cup of coffee from the cafeteria machine.

He couldn't believe this was happening. Courtney had gone to the doctor on Monday. He said she was doing fine and had gained two more pounds. The baby's heartbeat was strong. Her color was good, and no swelling showed in her ankles.

He took the coffee black, though he usually put sugar in machine coffee. It was always so acidic, but this time he needed the bitterness to stay awake. It might be a long night.

Slouching in a plastic chair, Steven stared at the coffee. He loved Courtney so very much. When she hurt, he hurt. He knew how much she counted on having their baby, how much Alice had prayed. Now this.

"Lord, if I could do anything, anything at all, I'd do it in a flash. Losing the baby would be devastating for her. To discover her birth mother is no longer living, losing her father at a young age—this is enough. Don't give her any more."

He drained the cup, squashed it in his hand, and tossed it into the nearest receptacle. If only he understood things better. If only Grams—who'd raised him to be a believer—had explained that part to him. How did you protect someone you loved with all your heart? How did you keep bad things from happening to them?

A janitor, sweeping the floor, looked over. "Are you okay?"

Steven nodded. "Yeah. My wife's in emergency. Guess I'd better get back."

When he entered the room, Alice looked up with pain-filled eyes. Courtney appeared to be sleeping.

Dr. Blanton, the gynecologist, had come in. "The ultrasound shows it's what I suspected. The best condition would be if the baby stayed in the uterus a few more weeks, but if bed rest doesn't help and the bleeding continues, we'll need to perform a cesarean section."

Alice called Leighton from the hospital. For once she hoped the answering machine would pick up because she was afraid she might start crying when she heard his voice.

He answered on the third ring.

"Leighton, I had to let you know—Courtney's in the hospital." Then she couldn't talk.

"Alice? Alice, speak to me."

Steven, assessing the situation, grabbed the phone. He explained what had happened and that they had every reason to hope she could carry the baby longer.

Alice ran out into the hall to cry. It wasn't good for Courtney to see her upset. Besides, she didn't know what to do with herself.

Steven joined her in the hallway. "Leighton says he's coming to town."

"He can't."

"But he will." Steven put an arm around Alice. "Don't you know by now that men feel protective about the women they love?"

She looked up. "He doesn't love me."

"He doesn't? You mean he hasn't said it in so many words?"

Alice looked down at her knotted tissue. It was in shreds, and she dug for another in the pocket of her jacket.

"You think about it, Alice. If you start putting two and two together, you'll come up with the answer. Now, I must sit with Courtney."

Alice paced back and forth, wondering about what Steven said. She wasn't sure she loved Leighton, but if wanting him here now, if wanting him to share the ups and downs was any indication, she guessed—no—she *knew* she loved him and couldn't imagine giving him up.

&

He never doubted that he'd drive to the city. It didn't matter that it was three in the morning; he had to go. And as he drove over the miles, he realized he had come to a crossroads. He'd battled it. Tried to look the other way. Did everything in his power to ignore the facts. Then when he'd talked to Luke and today when he'd heard from Aaron, things had come together. God's timing, he knew.

Alice was hurting, and he hurt because she hurt. He was in

love with her. He'd tried to deny it more than once. He listened to people talking, his sons suggesting he cool it, that he look for someone closer, someone who understood what life was like in a place like Oysterville. And he knew it would be hard doing what he had to do. He'd mulled it over in his mind a hundred times, set his plan into motion by discussing the business with Luke. Now that Aaron was coming, they could work the business together. Maybe Aaron would like to take over the store operation, fill orders, and look for more products.

Now he couldn't wait to see Alice. As he sped over the miles he slipped *Fiddler* into the player. He needed something to lighten up the situation, so he sang, "If I were a rich man."

twenty-one

Dr. Blanton suggested Courtney stay until morning. "I want you to be closely supervised. We have a wonderful staff here. They'll alert me should you start hemorrhaging again. And if you have even one contraction, I want to know immediately." He smiled as he patted Courtney's arm. "For now, stop worrying."

"Celia," he called to a nurse. "Put her on an IV. I don't want to take a chance of dehydration."

"Yes, Doctor, right away."

"When can she come home?" Steven asked.

"If all goes well, tomorrow. I'll make rounds around ten. I'll make a decision then." The doctor paused in the doorway. "Since there's plenty of room, we'll just keep you here. If things change, you'll be up on the third floor."

"There's only one solution," Alice said, after Dr. Blanton had left. "Courtney should come to my house. I can take better care of her there. She can have my bedroom, since obviously she shouldn't climb the stairs."

"Mom, I can sleep in the nursery."

"No. You need the larger bed. I'll take the single bed in the nursery."

Steven nodded as he kissed Courtney's forehead. "We're going to have a fine, healthy son," he said. "And if he should come by cesarean, that's what will happen."

Alice hugged her son-in-law. "God bless you, Steven. I need someone with positive thinking right now."

"I just pray for no contractions," Courtney said. "It sounds as if that will be the deciding factor."

The nurse looked in. "Why don't you all try to get some rest?"

"Yeah. I can sleep sitting up," Steven said. "I've done that before."

Alice dozed fitfully as she sat to one side of the bed, while Steven sat in the other chair, holding his wife's hand.

Someone cleared his throat from the hall. "The nurse told me where to find you."

Alice jerked awake and saw Leighton. Smiling, she rushed to his side. "You came."

He put an arm around Alice. "Wild horses couldn't have kept me away. And I want you to know it's going to be okay. We have the whole peninsula praying. I called Luke before I left."

Tears formed in Alice's eyes. Leighton tightened his arm around her. "I thought you could use some support about now. So what does the doctor say?"

"We just have to keep her quiet and in bed," Steven said.

Courtney opened her eyes. "Thank you for coming. I always wanted to be lazy."

"Don't listen to her," Alice said. "She makes an awful patient, believe me."

"We're hoping she can go home in the morning." Steven glanced at Leighton. "Man, you look like you could use some coffee. I'll show you where the machines are, unless you want me to bring you some."

"No, I'll go with you."

"So how's it really going?" Leighton asked once they were out of earshot.

"I think we got a warning in the nick of time." Steven ran his hand through his hair. "The baby may have to be taken, but the doctor is hoping to wait a few more weeks, at least."

"This is so hard on Alice."

"I know."

Leighton found a cinnamon bun to go with the coffee. "What did they do, sprinkle a little cinnamon on cardboard?"

Steven laughed. "I see you haven't had much of hospital vending machine goodies."

Shaking his head, Leighton said, "No, not since my Hannah was so sick."

"Yeah, heard about that. I'm sorry."

"God doesn't shut the sun out every day."

The two men walked back. When Leighton was confident that everything was okay, he left for his son's.

As he drove across town to John's high-rise, Leighton wondered if he really knew what Alice felt. Would there be room in her life for him? Was he going to matter to her? He read something in her eyes, felt something in her touch, but was it enough?

"Lord, You know my prayer and I know You hear me. Help me to accept what Your will is in this. Help me to be there for Alice, but to be patient, too."

When John didn't answer the doorbell after several rings, Leighton suddenly wished that he'd remembered the key. The door finally swung open, and John stared. "Dad! What are you doing here?"

"It's a bit of a story. Can I come in?"

"Well, sure. I just wasn't expecting you to come calling at seven A.M."

"Aren't you going to work?"

"Well, yes, but as you know, when you own your own business, you can be late sometimes." He rubbed his eyes. "I repeat, why are you here?"

"I drove in to be with Alice. Her daughter is in the hospital. She might lose the baby."

"Oh, no. That's awful."

"I'll be sticking around for awhile. That is, if I can stay until I find another place."

"*Here?* You're moving to Portland?"

"I'm moving toward that, yes. I take it you haven't talked to Luke, then." Leighton slumped into the nearest chair.

"No, but I've been working late. Trying to get ready for the poinsettia orders. The biggest sale is the Friday after Thanksgiving."

"My son, we're both growing things. You flowers, me oysters."

John went into the kitchen and poured water into a coffee-pot. "I gotta have my caffeine. Then we need to talk."

"Talk?" It seemed like that was all he'd done lately.

"I think it's fine that you found someone to go out with you when you come to town, but why don't you leave it at that?"

Leighton eyed his second youngest son. "That's easy for you to say. You've never been married or even shown any indication you have anyone on the horizon. You obviously don't love someone."

"Dad, you went that route once."

"And does that mean I can't find love again because I'm *old?*"

"I didn't mean that."

"That's what it sounds like." Leighton poured himself a cup of coffee. "Now, do you have any bread to toast or cereal? I'm famished. I'm also finished discussing this."

After John left for work, Leighton took a short nap. Then he checked and discovered Courtney had been discharged. He headed over to Alice's, stopping first for a bouquet of pink roses and yellow carnations.

"Leighton!" Alice looked surprised yet pleased. "I'd hoped to see you again before you left." She went in search of a vase.

"Remember the decision I talked about the other day?"

She nodded. "Yes, but you were so secretive."

"I'm moving here. To Portland. I'll be staying with John for a while, maybe help him out with his business."

Her eyes widened. "What do you mean?"

"I want to be here with you. I've already talked to Luke about things, and he's willing to run the business."

"Moving *here?*" Alice stopped arranging the flowers. "Maybe we both better sit down."

"I've given Luke full reins in the business, for the time being. I need to be near you, to see you every day. I think we should get married." The minute he said it, he wished he could take the words back. This wasn't the best way to propose marriage. He hadn't been romantic at all. Now that he thought about it, he realized he'd never said he loved her. Her eyes looked almost glazed.

"What did you mean when you said you gave Luke full reins in the business?"

"I said I was going on an extended vacation from my business."

"You did this because of me?"

"Yes. Is that surprising?"

Alice's eyes filled with tears again. "I guess it shouldn't be, but it is." She reached over and took his hand. "I guess when God's guiding your life, nothing He does should be amazing."

"I love you," he said in a thick voice. "I've loved you since that afternoon I first saw you. I hadn't even been praying to meet anyone. It just happened, with God's timing. Sometimes He kinda zaps you when you least expect it."

"But you can't move here, Leighton. It wouldn't work out."

"Why not?"

Alice moved her hand. "I can't let you do it. If I agreed to this move, you'd regret it. The bay is in your blood. Your work is there—your home, the cannery. I can't let you give that up."

"My mind's made up. I'm going to do it."

"And I say it's wrong." Her voice rose as she looked away. She couldn't look him in the eye. Not now.

"Are you saying you won't marry me, then?"

Alice got up and walked across the room. "I guess I am, Leighton. I don't want to give up my home here. It's my life. My family. You know that, so it wouldn't be right for me to ask it of you."

"I'm offering it."

"Oh, Leighton, I think not. It seems we're at an impasse."

"That's it, then? You're giving up on the whole idea of us being together?" He stalked to the door. "I thought this was what you wanted, too. I guess I was wrong."

She didn't answer.

He opened the door then turned around. "I'll be at John's, if you want to call."

She watched as he hurried up the walk. She wanted to cry out for him to come back but couldn't. As tears ran down her cheeks, she knew God would help her get over this obstacle as well as all the others she'd had in her life.

🙚

Leighton drove to the nearest drive-through and ordered a cup of the strongest coffee they made.

"Maybe you want a double shot of espresso, Sir."

"Make it a triple shot," he said.

He took the hot beverage, found a place with time on the parking meter, and stared at the Willamette.

"I've never wanted much, Lord," he said aloud. "I've tried to live a good life, be a good husband, father, son—not necessarily in that order. It seems things always happen to me, or as some would say, I've been at the wrong place at the wrong time. But you know, Lord, I wouldn't trade a day of it for anything else. I can't imagine not having had Hannah in my life or knowing Alice for these past few months. Maybe You'd have me go back to Oysterville and take care of my business, after all."

He finished the coffee and got out, putting the cup in the nearest trash can. Then he drove across the Morrison and on his way to John's to get his overnight bag. He'd never even unpacked.

twenty-two

Alice felt like a displaced woman. She had given up her volunteer job, the position with Spencer Consultants, and worst of all, had sent Leighton on his way. It had been a week since he'd returned to Oysterville, but it seemed like months. He sent E-mail on a daily basis, but the phone calls stopped. And inside her was an emptiness, but she couldn't think about it. All concern was with Courtney and keeping her stress-free.

Courtney had settled into a routine, and though Alice felt her daughter was doing well, she knew that she worried about her condition.

"Mom, what if I lose the baby?"

"You're not going to, so there."

"Are you going to visit Leighton soon?"

"I can't now."

"I don't want to see you moping around."

"Have I been moping?"

Courtney leaned up on an elbow. "Yes, Mom, you have. And it makes me think about the Scripture where it talks about a woman leaving her family and cleaving to her husband to build a new home. And that's what Steven and I are doing. Now you must build a new life for yourself with Leighton. We're going to be fine."

Alice felt her heart race at the thought. She hated that he hadn't called. She missed hearing his voice more than she'd ever imagined.

"I wonder if you shouldn't talk to the pastor about this to get some fresh insight."

Alice knew what her daughter was trying to do, but it wouldn't work. She'd decided that Leighton's place was in Oysterville, doing the work he loved, the work he'd always done. He'd be miserable in the city. After six months, maybe less, he'd be climbing the walls. No, she was certain she'd made the right decision by sending him home. He'd find someone. There was always Cora.

"It's better this way."

"Is it really?" Courtney set her embroidery down. Since she'd become bedfast, needlepoint and embroidery—which she'd put aside after marrying Steven—now came out of the sewing basket. "Don't you think God wants you happy?"

"Of course, Honey. God wants only the best for His children. I've always believed that."

Courtney reached for a strand of blue floss and threaded a needle. "Then if that's true, don't you think He had a hand in your meeting Leighton like you did? He could have had his laptop fixed on a day you were volunteering at the hospital."

Alice nodded. "Yes, that's true."

"So I think it was ordained that you two meet and fall in love."

"Why couldn't I have found someone closer?"

Courtney set her work aside again. "I don't know. But according to the Bible, we're not supposed to know all the answers."

"I know that, Honey, but I just can't even consider leaving you now."

"I think I understand." She reached over and took her mother's hand. "I wouldn't want you to. But I'm wondering if Auntie doesn't need to be doing something about now. She could come to stay with me for two or three days while you go down to the coast."

"I'll think about it."

Alice left the room then and got out the makings for cookies. She always baked when she had to work through a problem. She would make something chocolate, Courtney's favorite.

When she had the first batch in the oven and Courtney was napping, Alice turned on the computer. There probably wouldn't be any messages today. Should she send him a card? Yes, she wanted to do that. She'd tried to shut it out of her mind, but she knew she'd never forget the hurt look in his eyes or the way he'd turned and walked out the door, closing it softly behind him. She could still hear the sound of his car driving off.

She clicked on the letter icon and saw the number on the screen, announcing she had a card to open. She closed the door so Courtney wouldn't hear the music as she brought it up.

Dozens of colorful hearts were scattered across the screen. The message floated, and it was as if Leighton were in the room whispering in her ear. "I think of you every moment of every day and am still hoping you'll change your mind. Leighton."

She printed it out and added it to her growing notebook.

"Mom—" The door opened and Courtney peered in. "I thought so. You're checking E-mail, and I think the cookies are burning."

"Oh, no!" Alice raced down the hall, and the burned smell filled the kitchen. "I've never burned cookies in my life," she said, grabbing a pot holder.

"And you haven't been in love for a very long time," Courtney said.

"You go back and lie down, young lady!"

Alice scraped the burned rounds into the garbage and plopped into a chair. So much for concentration.

Courtney stood, arms folded. "Mom, I can't let you do this."

"Do what?"

"You know what I mean." She patted her rounded stomach. "I already called Auntie last night when you went to the store."

"You did?"

"Yes, and she can come. So you can get away and go back to the peninsula to see Leighton and get this cleared up."

"There's nothing to clear up."

"Mother, give me some credit for brains. You're in love with him, and he obviously adores and worships the ground you walk on."

"You can't say that."

Courtney looked exasperated. "And who made the trip here

in the middle of the night? Ask Steven. See what he says."

"Agnes really agreed to come stay with you?"

"Yes. And I want you to go. I mean it. I can't believe it's over. I think you two need each other, though I admit I was a bit jealous at first."

"You were jealous? I just thought you didn't want me to marry again."

"I know. After mulling it over, I knew I was being selfish."

"Oh, Honey, I had no idea."

"Now, Auntie is coming, so I think you have a trip to plan."

Alice's hopes soared. "You really think I should do this, and you don't mind having Agnes here?"

Courtney laughed. "Would I have brought it up if I did?"

Alice felt better after speaking to Agnes. "I can't say I agree with what you're doing, Alice, but guess it isn't up to me to judge, now, is it?"

"I'll have the cell phone," she told Courtney, "so if anything should happen, I want to know immediately. That's why it's better if I drive my car."

She didn't think of how she hadn't wanted to drive the night she got news that Courtney was in the hospital. But now she felt everything was under control. No more spotting. No contractions. The last doctor's appointment had gone well. And Courtney stayed calm and had complete bed rest. This would give Agnes a chance to feel needed.

Alice decided not to tell Leighton she was coming, though she alerted Trudy that she would need her old room.

"Is everything okay with you two?" Trudy said.

Alice swallowed hard. "Well, maybe not exactly, and that's why I'm coming up. And, Trudy, I want to surprise Leighton."

"Okay, Honey, whatever you think."

Alice packed just a few things, not knowing if she'd stay more than one day. Leighton might not want her anymore. Maybe he and Cora were a twosome. She certainly couldn't blame him. She didn't want to wait until morning but knew she must. It was going to be another sleepless night.

twenty-three

The autumn day couldn't have been nicer or more mellow. Alice was glad Courtney insisted on the trip. Things *had* been up in the air. She hadn't meant to hurt Leighton but knew she had. He'd risked his heart, and she'd all but shattered any dream he had of their building a life together.

She drove over the now-familiar route and stopped in Clatskanie for coffee and a break to stretch her legs. It was the halfway point. She liked to walk down by the river that ran through the town. Sipping her take-out coffee, she sat on a bench and contemplated her decision. She kept vacillating. One minute she was going to tell Leighton she'd changed her mind and she'd move to Oysterville and be his wife. The next minute she knew she could never do it, just as she could never expect him to move to the city.

A light breeze ruffled her hair and she remembered the many hikes she and Leighton had enjoyed. He had always been so gentle, protective of her. How could she not spend the rest of her life with him?

It was two o'clock when she arrived at the bed and breakfast. After Trudy carried her bag up the stairs, Alice freshened up a bit, then got back into the car. She could hardly wait to see Leighton now.

Trudy came out, waving her hands. "Dear, I just wanted you to know that Cora's at Leighton's house."

"Cora's at the house?"

"It's not what you think, I'm sure. She just probably finagled a way to go help clean. I know her."

Alice felt a sinking sensation. If Cora was there, she certainly wouldn't welcome the sight of Alice. Maybe she'd better stop by the cannery first.

Luke was the first person she saw. His face registered shock as he hurried over. "Alice! What are you doing here?"

"I must speak with Leighton. We had words before he left Portland the last time, and I just need to talk to him."

"He's in the store. I'll tell him you're here."

Alice went back to her car, wondering if she'd find the right words to convey her regrets at hurting him. That had never been her intention.

Leighton walked out the door of the Sea Gifts Store and headed toward her. His gait was purposeful, and her heart knew at that moment how much she loved this man. How much she wanted to be a wife to him. She got out of the car.

"Alice? Why are you here? How's Courtney?" He looked concerned.

"Courtney's fine. The last checkup showed the baby is in good condition. They may do a C-section at eight months."

"But, why are you here?" he repeated.

Alice felt compelled to gaze into his dark, haunting eyes. "Agnes is there. She'll do fine for a day or so."

"And then?"

Alice swallowed hard. "And then Courtney will have the baby, and—"

Leighton's gaze never wavered. "And then what? I'm waiting for that part. Do I move to Portland as I suggested, or are you coming here?"

"Well, I—" Again she couldn't find the words she wanted to say. Why was this so difficult?

"I can't keep going on like this. I'm the type of guy who needs to know point-blank where he stands. I know that the sun is going to come up in the morning and it's going to go down each night. I need to know if I can come home to the woman I love with all my heart and know she's there, body and soul, wanting to be with me and not pining away, wishing she were somewhere else."

"I'm trying to say what's in my heart." She wanted him to take her into his arms, to tell her everything was going to be all right, but he stood erect, staring at her, not saying what she'd hoped to hear. "I was wrong in sending you home like that. I hurt you, I know. I hurt us. I've come to apologize, Leighton. I can't get you out of my mind, and I just had to see you, to try to explain."

A car pulled up, and Alice saw it was Cora. Did she and Leighton have something going on? Had Trudy known and been afraid to tell her?

Cora rolled down the window. "Leight, I'm going across the river for that order. Did you have anything else to add to the list?"

She never said hello to Alice, as if she were invisible.

Leighton went over and leaned on the car. Alice wanted to disappear. Why had she thought this would work? She'd hurt him so much. How could this be happening? She'd loved and lost.

Alice started to get into her car, but he stopped her as Cora drove off.

"I have to know, Alice. No in-between for me. Perhaps it's better this way."

"Yes," she said woodenly. "Perhaps it is."

"How long will you be here?"

She swallowed hard. "I'll probably leave early in the morning."

She went back to Trudy's, holding the tears in check, but once she got to the privacy of her bedroom, she let them fall. Moments later, a tap sounded at the door.

"Alice? I have tea and some cranberry scones. Do you feel like company?"

"Yes, I do."

"So," Trudy said, setting the tray on the corner table. "I take it you saw Leighton."

"And Cora."

"You jumped to conclusions about Cora, I see."

"She's helping him run the show."

"Of course. That's what she wants. Are you ready to stand

by and let it happen?"

Alice stirred her tea mechanically. "He wants an answer from me, an answer I don't have."

"What part of 'yes' don't you understand?"

"There are too many entanglements in my life. Leighton can't handle that. He as much as said so."

"Poppycock! He's trying to conceal the hurt. That man's been through a fog thicker than any I've ever seen hit the bay."

"Cora's the one who can help him through."

"May I remind you that he doesn't love Cora."

"He can grow to love her."

"So you're giving up just like that?" The older woman snapped her fingers. "Frankly, I thought you had more starch in your backbone."

"Trudy, I just feel so overwhelmed."

"Leighton will be by. Later. Count on it. I think I'll make that meat loaf he likes so well."

Alice offered to help. She peeled potatoes, sliced onions, tore greens for a salad. She had to keep busy. It kept her mind from mulling over the situation.

They waited, but Leighton hadn't come by six, nor by seven. At seven-thirty Trudy said they'd better eat. "I'll not call him. It's up to him. What I know is there's a hurting man out there, and he needs time, Alice. Just give him time."

❧

Leighton, still shaken by Alice's presence, left work early. He'd had to restrain himself to keep from rushing to her, from taking her into his arms and telling her how much he loved her, how glad he was to see her. It had taken courage for her to come, for her to leave Courtney. And she'd done it. Why, then, had he been aloof? And why had Cora come at that precise moment? He'd seen the hurt in Alice's eyes and knew what she must be thinking.

When he entered the house, he glanced around, noticing the neatness. Cora had stopped by one day at work, insisting she needed a part-time job until something else opened up.

He'd said she could come out twice a week to clean. She kept it dusted and vacuumed, and there were clean dishes from the dishwasher again. The refrigerator held dinners and leftovers from previous meals.

Fresh wildflowers graced the table. His daily newspaper was on the nightstand beside his recliner. The *TV Guide* was opened to the right day. Why hadn't he noticed this before? Why did it hit him now?

He changed into clean slacks and a shirt. A photo of Nancy sat on the chest of drawers in his bedroom. Not that he ever noticed it, but he supposed he'd kept it there for the children's sake. He never wanted them to forget their mother. He touched the glass covering her face. It was free of dust. That meant Cora had to have dusted in his room every day she was here.

He put the photo back and thought again about his life. In spite of the sorrow, there'd been lots of joy. Even with Aaron running off, Leighton liked remembering the youngest son with the lock of hair that hung down on his forehead, the laughing eyes, the stubborn streak that got him into trouble. Now he'd been found and they'd be reunited soon.

In the refrigerator he found spaghetti and meatballs and half of a lemon meringue pie. He'd have a bit of both.

The sun had left the hills, and the room suddenly felt chilly. The house was big, way too much house for just himself. Why was he staying on here?

Cora enjoyed keeping his house. But she was also stubborn and bossy. If they married, she would run every aspect of his life. He'd been taking care of himself, but then Alice had entered his life and his heart. He hadn't wanted to let her in, but somehow she had.

He heard the car in the driveway and knew it was Cora. He'd expected her to come. It was just her way, and he knew her ways far too well. He'd let her into his life as well, and she'd mollycoddled him, making him think he needed her around.

"Leighton, I didn't think you'd be here." She was breathless, and he noticed she wore a dress, a frilly thing with lace.

"Then why did you come?"

She sat next to him on the love seat. "I guess I hoped you would be."

"Cora." He leaned forward. "We need to talk."

"Yes?" Her eyes shone.

"It isn't going to work, and you know it."

"What isn't?"

"You and me. Getting together. Marrying. Whatever it is that you want. I admire you tremendously, but I don't love you. I think we've been down this road before."

"It's that Alice!" She shot to her feet. "I don't know why she just doesn't stay in Portland. Everyone thinks we make a great couple. Ask Luke. Tom. Your daughters-in-law."

"It doesn't matter what they think. It matters what I think, what I feel."

"Alice doesn't know what a man needs. If she did, she'd have moved here by now."

He shook his head. "Alice is going through a lot right now. It's taking her time to sort things out."

"I'm not giving up, Leighton. I told you that before." She stood by the door, her hand on the knob. "I'll not come by until you call."

"Cora, will you wait a minute?"

She paused.

"Why did Meredith send Alice a threatening letter?"

Cora's hand fell at her side. "How did you—?"

Leighton chuckled. "Steven, Alice's son-in-law, told me. He E-mailed her and warned her about it being against the law to harass someone."

"It was just a joke."

"Yeah, sure."

"She doesn't deserve you, Leighton."

And you do? he wanted to say, but didn't.

"And another thing's been bothering me. Why did you take the photos out of the albums and put them in a box?"

She shrugged. "I just liked looking at all of you and, oh, I don't know why!"

"I'm sorry, Cora, but I've said that before, haven't I?"

"Yes, you have." She looked away. "I'm leaving now, but I'll wait for your call, and call you will. Alice isn't meant for this kind of life. Remember her coming in the first time in those ridiculous-looking gold high-heeled sandals? She won't survive. When you come to your senses, as Luke says you will, I'll be waiting. Remember, it's the little cottage at the end of Territory Road. The one with the white picket fence along the front."

He remembered, all right, but said nothing. The door closed softly, and her car started. Soon the sound died away. Leighton sat as if in a stupor and wondered why he thought he could ever control his life. For a man of fifty-three, he wasn't doing a very good job of it. As he watched the lights flickering from across the bay, he wondered what he was going to do next.

twenty-four

After dinner Alice went to the Garden Room, her home away from home. Her heart was heavy. Leighton hadn't come. Nor had he called. That made his feelings clear. Sometimes love wasn't enough. Loving a person didn't always make a relationship work. She knew Leighton had loved his first wife, but it hadn't been enough. How could he risk it again?

She didn't belong here any more than he belonged in Portland. "Your life is in Oysterville," she'd told him. "Having coffee at that little corner café."

He had agreed, finally, and written in an E-mail, "Yes, I expect you're right. If I'd wanted to find someone, I would have looked here first."

It was the wisest move for both. How could either uproot a life? Alice thought about Carl and all the traveling they'd done while he was in the air force. She'd survived that, hadn't she? It had been fun then, packing up, going to a new location, never knowing what to expect. But she'd been young. At fifty she considered things twice. No running into a relationship without thinking of possible consequences. Thank heavens she and Leighton were smart enough to realize that.

She felt a tear slide down her cheek and brushed it aside. She wouldn't cry. She'd leave first thing in the morning. There was no point in staying now.

Since she'd only brought one change of clothes, Alice didn't have much to pack. It would only take her five minutes. But while she put her few toiletry items in the small bag, she couldn't seem to stop the flow of tears. If Leighton loved her, he would have come over by now. They'd parted so badly. She could still hear the sound of his voice—so flat and clipped—when he'd left. A lump lodged in Alice's throat at the memory of her refusal. What she'd said hadn't been true. With every expression, every action, and every time he touched her, she wanted to be with him forever.

Alice set her suitcase on the floor then reached for her journal. She wrote a few lines, then looked at the inscription of the day. "Consider it pure joy, my brothers, whenever you face trials of many kinds, because you know that the testing of your faith develops perseverance."

Alice turned to the first chapter of James. She'd always loved this verse. But it was what came later that spoke to her heart now. "But when he asks, he must believe and not doubt, because he who doubts is like a wave of the sea, blown and tossed by the wind."

The Bible closed as it slipped from her grip. "Lord, are You telling me not to have doubts? That I should believe in this possible relationship, that I should have done or said something to let him know how I truly felt?"

Trudy tapped on the door. "Alice, I'm having a bout with loneliness. Can you come and have a spot of tea with me?"

It had only been an hour since they'd eaten, and Alice knew it was Trudy's way of trying to make her feel better.

"I'll be right down," Alice answered.

Trudy was in the parlor. "I'm all caught up on the work around here and there's not a decent program on the TV. Here. Have some shortbread. I just made them yesterday."

Alice laughed. "Guess you didn't want me to miss my sister. She always has shortbread on Sundays when Courtney and I go to visit."

She looked up and smiled. "That so?"

"Agnes is probably going to gloat and say she could have told me so. I mean, about this happening with Leighton."

"Sisters can be a blessing, but they can also be a pain in the neck," Trudy said. "I was never so blessed."

The two women chatted about their earlier lives and how they came to believe, how their faith had sustained them, and how they knew it would go on sustaining them.

"I would marry in a minute," Trudy said, "if someone should come along, but I firmly believe there is only one man for a woman. I had my one chance in a lifetime, and I thank God for the twenty-two years we had."

Alice had heard other women say that, but she didn't believe it. She felt there could be more than one match in a person's lifetime.

Trudy got up and closed the drapes. "What time are you fixing to leave tomorrow?"

"I think five would be good. I'll hit Portland after most everyone's gone to work. I hate driving in rush-hour traffic."

"I'll be up to make the coffee and get some muffins baked."

"No—" Alice reached out. "Please don't bother with that. I'll pick up coffee at one of the drive-thrus."

It wasn't a good night. At least not for sleeping. Alice loved the large bed, the fat feather pillows, and the view out the window. Leighton lived on the same bay that her room overlooked. A full moon cast a glow on the night's edges. She wondered if he might be looking out his window, gazing at the moon also. Or had he already forgotten about her and was busy watching a favorite TV program?

She felt tears press against her eyelids, but she couldn't give in to them. She was returning to Portland, going home and awaiting the birth of her first grandchild. Life couldn't get much better than that.

❧

Alice slipped down the stairs at five o'clock. It was still dark and damp, while the first traces of dawn filtered through the tall firs. She was going to miss this quiet, relaxing place. By the time she reached the Astoria Bridge, the first glorious rays from the rising sun would guide her way.

Trudy was awake, and she handed Alice a small box lunch. "For the road, my dear. But do stop to stretch once. I'll be praying for you." The two hugged and Alice quickly got into the car. She started backing out of the parking spot and nearly hit a Chevy truck.

Leighton! Had he come to say good-bye? She trembled as she pulled back into the spot. He roared into the driveway and was out of the truck before she had the engine shut off.

"You can't leave without my seeing you." The dark eyes held such intensity that her heart thudded.

"Get out of the car," he commanded, opening the door and touching her arm. "I didn't hold you yesterday, and I have to hold you just once more, to feel you in my arms, to just breathe in your fragrance. Oh, Alice—"

And then she was in his hard embrace, and the tears threatened again. This time she couldn't stop them, and as they fell against the wool of his coat, she felt his rough fingers brushing them away, then taking a handkerchief from his pocket.

"Don't cry. I can't bear to see a woman cry, especially not the woman I love."

"Leighton, we've been through this—" But his mouth got in the way and she couldn't finish the sentence.

She felt herself melt against the thick chest and felt his hands in her hair, taking out the ribbon she wore. "I love you, Alice, and I'm not going to let you just walk out of my life. I know what happened yesterday, the harsh words spoken in Portland. I've gone over my doubts so many times, but I know where your heart is, and I also know that where you are, I've got to be or I'll die."

"Oh, Leighton, I love you."

"Oh, Sweetheart. I love you, too."

"But—"

"Hear me out. I say we compromise. I'll help John out in his nursery a few months in Portland, then you can come here with me for a few months in Oysterville."

"Do you think that would work?"

"We're at the age when we can make it work. Anytime you want, go down to be with your kids. And why not let Courtney and Steven have the house and we'll use one of the spare bedrooms upstairs when we come to visit? I think it's a dandy idea."

Alice felt her hopes rise as she gazed into Leighton's eyes. She took in his strong, determined chin, his thick hair, and knew, yes, it would work because with God's help, they would *make* it work.

The front door of the bed and breakfast opened. "Will you two come in out of the cold?" Trudy yelled. "I have fresh coffee made and hate to see a pot go to waste."

Leighton shut Alice's car door, then closed the door of his truck. Arm in arm, they trudged up the steps and into the house.

epilogue

"Oh, Mom, I'm so excited at the prospect of going to Oysterville to see where you'll be living half of the year." Courtney's eyes were shining. "And the wedding will be beautiful."

"Made even more special with the arrival of Aaron last week. I haven't seen Leighton this happy since that morning at Trudy's when we knew we wanted to build a life together. Now give me that grandson so I can tell him how much his grandmother loves him."

Steven Carl felt good in her arms. He was healthy, now weighing ten pounds. In the six weeks since his birth, he had gained and progressed well, in spite of his being born a month early.

"You are one lucky baby," she cooed against his soft cheek.

"Mom, getting married in the Oysterville Church is such an awesome idea!"

"I think so, and of course, Leighton does, too. He has far more children and friends and neighbors there. The church here will throw a reception later."

Alice had to pinch herself every time she realized what was happening. In December she and Leighton would repeat vows. The church would be filled with bouquets of pink roses. A reception would be held at Oysterville's old schoolhouse.

Leighton was driving into town today. And together they would write out their wedding vows. As Alice cut a picture from a magazine, she knew her wedding dress would be the most beautiful thing she'd ever owned. White velvet with long sleeves and a scoop neckline. It would look lovely next to Leighton's tuxedo with a pink cummerbund.

Courtney, in a long pink organza gown, would be the matron of honor, and Luke would be his father's best man.

The telephone rang. It was Leighton.

"Is this the bride-to-be?"

Alice giggled. "I am, if this is the groom. Where are you now?"

"About five blocks away and can't wait to hold you in my arms again."

"Leighton, people will talk."

"Let them talk, anyway. You'd better be in the yard in about two minutes."

As Alice ran outside, she thanked God for answered prayer, for the happiness that welled up. It was going to be a wonderful life.

A Letter To Our Readers

Dear Reader:

In order that we might better contribute to your reading enjoyment, we would appreciate your taking a few minutes to respond to the following questions. We welcome your comments and read each form and letter we receive. When completed, please return to the following:

Rebecca Germany, Fiction Editor
Heartsong Presents
PO Box 719
Uhrichsville, Ohio 44683

1. Did you enjoy reading *The Sea Beckons* by Birdie L. Etchison?
   ❏ Very much. I would like to see more books
      by this author!
   ❏ Moderately
      I would have enjoyed it more if _____

   _____

   _____

2. Are you a member of **Heartsong Presents**? Yes ❏ No ❏
   If no, where did you purchase this book? _____

   _____

3. How would you rate, on a scale from 1 (poor) to 5 (superior), the cover design? _____

4. On a scale from 1 (poor) to 10 (superior), please rate the following elements.

   _____ Heroine   _____ Plot

   _____ Hero   _____ Inspirational theme

   _____ Setting   _____ Secondary characters

5. These characters were special because_____

_____

_____

6. How has this book inspired your life?_____

_____

_____

7. What settings would you like to see covered in future
   Heartsong Presents books?_____

_____

_____

8. What are some inspirational themes you would like to see
   treated in future books?_____

_____

_____

9. Would you be interested in reading other **Heartsong
   Presents** titles?   Yes ❑   No ❑

10. Please check your age range:
    ❑ Under 18   ❑ 18-24   ❑ 25-34
    ❑ 35-45   ❑ 46-55   ❑ Over 55

11. How many hours per week do you read?_____

Name _____

Occupation _____

Address _____

City _____ State _____ Zip _____

$\mathbb{W}$hat happens when fairy-tale adventures meet modern life? Find out in this unique novella collection, as four women hope for the "happily ever after" of a God-ordained marriage.

In *A Rose for Beauty*, feel Beauty Bartlett's pain over losing her home—and especially over having to work for the man who took it. Can she see past his scars to the person within, or will the loss of her family fortune forever be a thorn between them?

Marissa Jones has long been known as *The Shoemaker's Daughter*. Now her knowledge of the business may help to mend a rift between herself and the business's new owner. But will her secretive interference be appreciated?

In *Lily's Plight*, seven very different men will set Lily White's world spinning. Can she find her place in a new job environment, or will she run back home with a broken heart?

In *Better to See You*, a visit to her grandmother's home sets up Lucy Blake for a reunion with her old flame. Against the backdrop of this exciting development, how will she defend the old lady against a threat to her financial security?

Fairy tales can come true—enjoy the enchantment of these classic stories brought to life by authors Irene B. Brand, Lynn A. Coleman, Yvonne Lehman, and Gail Gaymer Martin.

paperback, 352 pages, 5 ³⁄₁₆" x 8"

♥ ♥ ♥ ♥ ♥ ♥ ♥ ♥ ❤ ♥ ♥ ♥ ♥ ♥ ♥ ♥ ♥

♥ ♥ ♥ ♥ ♥ ♥ ♥ ♥ ❤ ♥ ♥ ♥ ♥ ♥ ♥ ♥ ♥

·······Presents·······

Great Inspirational Romance at a Great Price!

Heartsong Presents books are inspirational romances in contemporary and historical settings, designed to give you an enjoyable, spirit-lifting reading experience. You can choose wonderfully written titles from some of today's best authors like Hannah Alexander, Irene B. Brand, Yvonne Lehman, Tracie Peterson, and many others.

When ordering quantities less than twelve, above titles are $2.95 each.
Not all titles may be available at time of order.

Hearts♥ng Presents
Love Stories Are Rated G!

That's for godly, gratifying, and of course, great! If you love a thrilling love story, but don't appreciate the sordidness of some popular paperback romances, **Heartsong Presents** is for you. In fact, **Heartsong Presents** is the *only inspirational romance book club* featuring love stories where Christian faith is the primary ingredient in a marriage relationship.

Sign up today to receive your first set of four, never before published Christian romances. Send no money now; you will receive a bill with the first shipment. You may cancel at any time without obligation, and if you aren't completely satisfied with any selection, you may return the books for an immediate refund!

Imagine. . .four new romances every four weeks—two historical, two contemporary—with men and women like you who long to meet the one God has chosen as the love of their lives. . . all for the low price of $9.97 postpaid.

To join, simply complete the coupon below and mail to the address provided. **Heartsong Presents** romances are rated G for another reason: They'll arrive *Godspeed!*